The man in the ski mask fled.

Seth watched two of the bull riders go after him. He gritted his teeth against the renewed throbbing in his leg and lifted his head to find Tonya headed toward him, tears streaming down her cheeks.

Bruises had already started to form on her throat, and rage ignited within him as Seth deduced what had happened. The man had broken in to her motor home with the intention of killing her.

Just like he'd tried to do four years ago.

Seth reached for her, and she stumbled into his arms to collapse against his chest. He wrapped his arms around her, balancing himself and her on his good leg. "Shh," he whispered against her ear. "It's all right. He's gone."

She clung to him a moment, her shoulders shaking, not making a sound. But he could feel the warmth of her tears soaking through his shirt. He held her, tried to offer her the comfort and safety she so desperately needed to feel.

She finally stirred and brushed a hand across her wet cheeks. "Are you all right? Your leg?" she whispered.

His heart shuddered. She was concerned about him when she'd been almost killed? He simply nodded. "I'm fine."

Lynette Eason is a bestselling, award-winning author who makes her home in South Carolina with her husband and two teenage children. She enjoys traveling, spending time with her family and teaching at various writing conferences around the country. She is a member of RWA (Romance Writers of America) and ACFW (American Christian Fiction Writers). Lynette can often be found online interacting with her readers. You can find her at facebook.com/lynette.eason and on Twitter, @lynetteeason.

Books by Lynette Eason

Love Inspired Suspense

Wrangler's Corner

The Lawman Returns
Rodeo Rescuer

Capitol K-9 Unit

Trail of Evidence

Family Reunions

Hide and Seek
Christmas Cover-Up
Her Stolen Past

Rose Mountain Refuge

Agent Undercover
Holiday Hideout
Danger on the Mountain

Visit the Author Profile page at Harlequin.com for more titles.

RODEO RESCUER

LYNETTE EASON

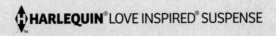

HARLEQUIN® LOVE INSPIRED® SUSPENSE

Recycling programs
for this product may
not exist in your area.

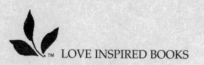

™ LOVE INSPIRED BOOKS

ISBN-13: 978-0-373-44691-9

Rodeo Rescuer

Copyright © 2015 by Lynette Eason

www.Harlequin.com

Printed in U.S.A.

Yea, though I walk through the valley of the shadow of death, I will fear no evil; For You *are* with me; Your rod and Your staff, they comfort me.
–Psalms 23:4

Dedicated to my family. I love you to pieces.

Acknowledgments

Special thanks to Jeff Thomas for answering
all of my questions about the rodeo circuit.
I appreciate it so much!
I take full responsibility for any mistakes.

ONE

If he caught her, he'd kill her. Tonya Waters hunched lower in the bullfighter barrel and held her breath.

Don't move. Don't make a sound. Don't even breathe. She closed her eyes and sent up a prayer. Would he look in the barrel? It seemed like such an obvious hiding place. Then again, it was one of many barrels in the equipment room. It would take him a while to search each one. Hopefully, she would be able to get out before he reached her.

But the footsteps moved closer to her. That sickening sweet cologne she remembered from four years ago tickled her gag reflex. She swallowed and curled into herself as tight as she dared. Her fingers, gripping the straps that had been mounted on the inside of the sphere, went numb.

"Tonya?"

His low singsong voice sent shivers of fear coursing through her. Stars danced before her eyes and she drew in another shallow breath. If she passed out, it was over. The stars faded. She lifted her head a fraction, just enough to see out of the top of the barrel.

Screams from the rodeo crowd just over her head reached her. Tonya had thought she'd be safe here, be a part of the rodeo, blend in with the crew. She'd been almost positive that the clown makeup and baggy clothes would be enough of a disguise should any pictures appear in a newspaper or on the news. Being a rodeo clown—or a bullfighter, as some were called—was hard work, exhilarating work.

Dangerous work.

But not as dangerous as having an obsessed ex-boyfriend finally track you down.

Now she'd have to run again. Change her name again. Find a new line of work.

Hank Newman had stalked her in college, threatened her family and nearly killed her. And now he'd come after her one more time. *God, help me!*

His good-looking exterior hid a heart of evil. Of violence and the potential to kill. Her throat tightened at the memory. He'd wrapped his fingers around her throat and pressed. Tight, tighter. Until she'd passed out. He'd dropped her to the floor and walked out, leaving her for dead.

She'd pressed charges and sent him to jail. And not even his powerful law-enforcement family could stop it. The fingerprints he'd left on her throat had matched his and a jury had put him away. But he hadn't stayed locked up for long. He'd shown up a few months later at her office, where she'd been working only a few weeks. Fortunately, she'd seen him before he'd seen her and she'd slipped out of the office without a backward glance, knowing she would never be safe as long as he was free.

And now he was here. Looking for revenge.

Her eyes closed, not wanting to remember the hate on his face in the courtroom. "I'll come after you, Tonya. You're mine. If I can't have you, no one will."

The whispered cliché often made her awaken drenched in a fear-induced sweat.

How had Hank found her? The question tumbled through her mind as her muscles began to cramp. She listened. He hadn't spoken a word except her name. She hadn't heard footsteps except the ones that had brought him next to her hiding place.

What was he *doing*?

Listening for her just as intently as she was listening for him.

Tears leaked down her cheeks.

A scraping sound against the floor brought her head up. Another scrape. More footsteps. A barrel rocking. Terror thundered through her. *No, no, no.*

He was searching the barrels.

She could *feel* him getting closer, heard him mutter something under his breath.

"Hey, what are you doing in here? This room is for approved personnel only."

Tonya jerked, then nearly cried in relief. She recognized Seth Starke's voice. A buckaroo. A tall, good-looking bull rider whose blue eyes she'd spent way too much time noticing lately. But one who had impeccable timing. *Thank You, Lord.*

"Uh, sorry. I took a wrong turn. I was, uh…looking for something," a voice said. Hank's voice, that deep bass that she'd just started to push from her memory. She'd know it anywhere.

"Well, come on out of there. What can I help you find?"

"The restroom?"

Seth snorted. "Try up the hall and on the right."

"Of course. Thanks."

Tonya listened to the fading footsteps and finally the door shut with a soft click. She let her muscles relax and winced at the pain as the blood began to flow once again. When she could, she stood and climbed out of the barrel on still-shaky legs, then shot a glance at the clock on the wall. She was going to be late.

Hank Newman was here. Frustration and terror clawed at her. She didn't want to run. She liked her life and what she'd built with the rodeo. But what other choice did she have?

But not until after Seth's ride. It was the last one of the day and then she'd be finished. Then she could plan her next move. But what would that be? Stay and fight back? Or head for the hills? She drew in a deep breath and headed for the door.

Then paused, her hand on the knob.

Was he there? Just outside? Waiting for her to step through so he could grab her and wrap his strong, menacing hands around her throat again?

Tremors shook through her. She leaned her head against the door and tried to calm herself. He wouldn't be there. Seth would have made sure of that. She turned the knob and shoved the door open.

The figure loomed in front of her. She let out a gasp and swallowed a scream.

"Hey, are you all right?" Seth grasped Tonya by the arm. She swayed and her stark white face troubled him. He'd admired her from afar for so long it felt strange to actually touch her.

She drew in a deep breath. "It's you."

"Yeah. Where did you come from? I didn't see you in there."

She gave him a shaky smile. "I was hiding." The little laugh she let escape didn't suggest she thought it was funny.

"Hiding? From...?"

"The guy you chased off. Thanks for that, by the way."

Seth frowned as warning bells went off in his mind. "Why were you hiding from him?"

"Doesn't matter now." She straightened and he realized he was still holding her upper arm. He let go and she tugged at the hem of her colorful long sleeve, fluffed the bright red wig and stuck her jaw out. "We're going to be late."

Seth followed her glance to the clock on the wall. She was right. They had to get going. "Are you sure you're up to this?" He was concerned. He wanted to know about the fear lingering in her eyes. Color had crept back into her cheeks, but she was still tense, glancing over his shoulder every few seconds as though she expected someone to walk up.

"I'm fine. Or I will be." Her blue gaze met his, and just like always, he felt drawn to her. She appeared fragile, yet he knew how strong she really was. And brave. No one could face down a thousand-pound bull and not have a spine of steel. That was why the fear in her eyes rattled him. Made him want to confront whatever had scared her. She gave him a light shove toward the men's dressing rooms. "I'll be out there in a minute."

"I'll wait."

She shook her head. "Go. You need to get ready. I'm on the way to the arena. I'll be right behind you."

Another glance at the clock sent urgency shooting through him. She was right—he'd have to hurry. "All right." He looked around. "I think that guy is gone."

"Good. Go. I'll be fine."

Seth hesitated one more second, then took off, his boots echoing against the concrete floor. He didn't know much about Tonya, just what he'd learned from working with her on an almost daily basis. But what he knew, he liked, and he vowed to make an effort to get to know her better. Soon. The fact that she was scared of the guy Seth had caught in the storage room really worried him. Not only did he vow to get to know Tonya better, he promised to be there for her if she needed him. For friendship, protection…or more.

Tonya watched Seth leave and reached out to grip the doorframe. Chills pebbled over her skin. Hank Newman had found her. For years she'd never stopped watching over her shoulder and today it had paid off. Sort of. She'd seen him before he'd seen her. He looked different, but she'd recognized him. Almost too late, but quick enough to get away from him.

Seth Starke had shown up at just the right time. And so had the attraction that she'd been noticing every time she found herself in Seth's presence. But she couldn't think about that right now.

Confusion flooded through her. What was Hank doing here? No, wrong question. She knew what he was doing here. The main question was: How had he found her?

Another quick look at the clock had her groaning. She wilted against the doorframe to give herself a few seconds to get it together. Finally, she straightened, scrutinized the few people hurrying toward the stairs that would lead up to the arena. She had a show to finish. Then she could figure out her next move.

Seth watched Mia Addison entertain the crowd with the two dogs who traveled with her wherever she went. They were great for filling up the downtime that happened between rides and events. Adults loved her show as much as the kids. Seth let his gaze wander the area. Where was Tonya? She'd said she'd be right behind him.

Tonya Waters. The woman who'd started to come to

mind more often than not. He'd thought he'd seen her slip into the supply room and had planned to grab a private moment to ask her out. Only he'd found another man following her.

Someone who'd scared her enough to send her into hiding. Just as he'd been about to open the door to the storage room and call out to her, she'd opened it herself. The sheer terror that had stared back at him for that brief moment before she realized it was him stayed with him and he planned to ask her about it as soon as he could.

He drew in a steadying breath and climbed the gate, balancing himself on the top rail. Soon he'd throw his legs over and drop onto the bull who pranced and snorted. He glanced up. Still no Tonya.

He'd noticed her from the moment he'd met her, but she'd belonged to someone else. Now she was single again, her boyfriend killed in a freak bullfighting accident. He'd heard through the grapevine that Tonya still blamed herself a year later. The sadness in her eyes drew him, made him want to offer comfort. Which was crazy. His eyes scanned the area again. His already tense muscles bunched harder. Had the guy who'd frightened her gone back to find her? Where *was* she?

As though in answer to his silent question, Tonya stepped into the arena, rolling her barrel. She wore loose-fitting clothes that would enable her to move freely and quickly. Underneath the brightly colored shirt, she wore a vest. The vest and the barrel would protect her—somewhat—if the bull came after her.

Seth shuddered to think of it, but she was a professional. She did her job so he could do his. He swung his legs over the rail fencing and settled himself on the back of the bull. Then he gathered the rosined rope near the bull's neck.

"You ready for this?" Jake Foster, one of Seth's good friends and another bull rider, asked.

"As ready as I'll ever be."

Jake, Seth Starke, Daniel Sanders and Monty Addison, Mia's brother, had been the four buckaroos. Until Daniel had died. Now it was the three of them, and while they fiercely competed against one another for the prize money, they were best friends who still mourned the loss of Daniel.

"We going out for drinks after this?" Jake asked.

"You know I don't drink."

"Come on, man. You know the strongest thing I'm talking about is a root beer."

Seth gave a low chuckle. He did know that. Jake was a recovering alcoholic and had been clean for five years. "We'll see how this ride goes."

"I'll even drive."

Seth snorted. "No way I'm getting in your trash heap." The man literally had garbage stacked to the ceiling in the backseat of his king cab. Drink cups, food wrappers, magazines and old newspapers. It had become a joke among the friends. No one would ride in Jake's truck for fear of getting lost amid the trash. Seth suspected the man did that on purpose. Sure saved him on gas money when he rode with someone else.

"I'll clean it out just for you."

"Right."

"Seriously, I'll—"

"It's okay, Jake. You don't have to try and take my mind off this ride. I need to focus."

"I know." His pal shut up and helped Seth settle in. Seth passed the rope between his pinkie and ring finger, then over the top of his hand across the back and around again to thread it under where it crossed his palm. Then he moved the rope between his middle and index fingers and clamped down hard.

He was ready.

No, he wasn't.

Fear flared. "Do you ever think about Daniel before you ride?" he asked through clenched teeth.

"Every time," Jake said. He'd watched his friend die just as Seth had. Then six months later, Seth had fallen and been horribly injured. He knew Jake had to wonder if he was next.

"Where's Monty?"

"He was on the computer in the break room last time I saw him. The orders are rolling in." Monty and several of the other buckaroos ran a side business selling Western wear through an online store. "Don't worry—he'll be here. Like you said…you just focus on staying on."

"Right." Focus would be a good thing. Staying on would be even better.

For Seth the flashes of falling off the bull six months ago wouldn't fade. He'd been back riding now for two months, training and working. And each time he got on one of the beasts, the images from the past came forward to taunt him. *Focus.*

Mia and her well-trained dogs ran from the arena to the resounding cheers and applause of the entertained audience. Mia used dogs, while Tonya defied death walking a high wire and being shot out of a cannon. Mia would be back in about fifteen seconds to help Tonya bull-fight.

The clock ticked. Mia returned in a flash of color and renewed applause. She moved opposite of Tonya and waited on the other side of the gate.

A third bullfighter, Rhett Jamison, grasped the rope he'd use to pull open the gate when Seth gave him the signal. Tonya met his gaze then gave him a slow nod. The timekeeper held the stopwatch next to Seth's head. He'd press the button as soon as the gate opened. His muscles bunched and he forced them to relax. He'd have to move with the bull, not fight him. He nodded to Rhett.

Rhett pulled the rope and the gate opened. The bull shot out and went into his rocking north-and-south bucking motion. Seth kept his free arm up, his stomach tight, his weight centered over the hand that gripped the rope, muscled legs clamped against the beast's sides.

Eight seconds. Just do it for eight seconds.

He knew what he was doing. The ride felt right. Good. The fear fled. Exhilaration filled him. He let his body flow with the movement. Time slowed; the roar of the crowd faded. It was just him and the bull.

The bell sounded. Elation zipped through him. He'd done it again. He'd stayed on. The rope slipped. He frowned and felt himself falling. No, this wasn't supposed to happen. Wha—?

Seth was on the ground, his lungs straining for air. The past rushed back to hit him and he steeled himself for the pain, for the bull to trample him. He tried to breathe, to roll, and couldn't move.

A hoof hit his newly healed leg. Pain ricocheted through him and blackness descended.

"Seth," Tonya whispered even as she, Rhett and Mia went into action. Mia moved, flapping her arms. The bull turned in her direction and galloped toward her. She ran for the barrel, then dived inside. The bull stopped and turned back to focus on Seth and the men who'd already jumped into the arena to grab him. But there was no way they'd get him over the fence in time if the bull charged.

Tonya raced forward, her brain whirling. She had to buy the men time. She yelled and snagged her horn from her pocket. A fierce blow loud enough to hurt her ears confused the animal. He stopped and turned to look at her for a brief second.

Then ignored her and charged back toward Seth. The men almost had him over the fence.

Tonya dashed over to slap the bull on his hindquarters, then dart off to the right since he had his head lowered and to the left. The animal roared, pivoted in the direction she'd anticipated he would. It bought her some time, but not much. He finally came after her. Mia, who'd climbed from the safety of her barrel, waved her hands and yelled, but the bull had Tonya in his sights and wasn't being distracted.

Tonya didn't hesitate. She was dead if she did. She ran for the fence, grasped the top rail and flipped herself over. She hit the ground on the other side as the bull's horns hooked through the fence. With a snort and a few bucks, he stomped off, back to the pen. Mia jumped over the fence and collapsed down on the ground. "You okay?"

"Yeah. You?"

"Yeah."

"I'm all right," Tonya gasped. "And Seth… Did they get him out? Is he okay?"

"Thanks to you, he is," a deep male voice said. Tonya felt hands grab her, pulling her to her feet, and immediately her mind went to her stalker. She released a quavering sigh. The man who had her was a stranger to her, but somewhere in the crowd, Hank Newman waited.

Was he still here? Her eyes darted from face to face. Too many faces. He could be hiding behind any one of them. "That was some move you did there over the rail. Never seen anything like it," another voice said.

Tonya focused on the speaker. Monty Addison, Mia's brother. "Gymnastics," she muttered. She took several long, deep breaths. "Where's Seth now? How bad is he hurt?" She whirled around, still scanning the area, grimacing at the twinge in her lower back. She might have made it over the fence, but her form could have used a little work.

She saw the EMTs hovering over Seth about ten yards down. She rushed toward him, concerned. "Please, God, let him be okay," she whispered.

Monty stayed with her. She could almost feel his worry as she came up to the edge of the crowd. They now had Seth on a stretcher, his leg in splints. The sight of his pale, colorless face grabbed her heart, and she nearly buckled as the past rose up in her mind once again. "Daniel," she whispered. "Not again."

"He's going to be all right, Tonya," Monty said, gripping her arm. "It's not like Daniel this time. Seth is going to be fine. Maybe banged up and sore, but okay."

She blinked back tears. "How do you know?"

"They didn't pull the sheet over his face." He turned and walked away.

Tonya swallowed hard. Daniel. Her friend, the man who'd wanted to marry her. Grief welled up again and she shoved it aside. The EMTs carried Seth through the silent crowd and to the ambulance. While they maneuvered him inside, she glanced around, eyes probing. Rhett gave her a two-fingered salute. She nodded and kept looking. Where was Hank? She didn't want to leave town just yet; she wanted to stay and find out how Seth was doing. But she couldn't take a chance that Hank would find her and try to kill her again.

She raced toward the ambulance and grabbed one of the EMTs' arms before he could swing into the driver's seat. "Let me go with him," she panted.

"Sorry, ma'am."

A glance over her shoulder sent terror slashing through her as her eyes collided with Hank Newman's. He lifted a hand and she saw his lips form the word *"Wait."*

She looked for an escape route. The crowd pressed in, so she couldn't run fast enough to get away from Hank. He would catch up to her. She did a one-eighty, eyes searching, desperation filling her. She looked back, made a split-second decision and leaped into the back of the ambulance just as the other EMT reached to close the door. "I have to go with him. Please."

"Who are you?"

"A friend," she said softly.

He studied her for a second. "Sorry."

"Let her come," Seth rasped.

The paramedic turned back to Seth. "You're awake?"

"Let her come." He let out a pained groan and rolled his head on the pillow. The EMT grasped his stethoscope. "Come on, then." He held out a hand.

She latched on to it and scrambled up into the nearest seat. She glanced back and saw Hank closing the distance. "Hurry," she pleaded.

"Tonya!"

She glanced left, panic-stricken, but that wasn't Hank calling her. Jake Foster sped toward her. He seemed dead set on stopping them before it was too late, but impatience to get the doors shut hurtled through her. Moments later Jake reached the back of the ambulance and tossed an object at her. She caught it in midair. A phone. "It's Seth's cell," he told her. "I want to be able to call. Keep it on. Tell him I'll clean out my truck if he needs a ride home from the hospital!" He disappeared as the doors slammed shut in his face. She shoved the phone in her back pocket and let a relieved breath escape her.

The EMT looked at her funny. She ignored him and

glanced at Seth. He still looked awful and she thought he might have lapsed back into unconsciousness. Within seconds they were moving. Through the back window, she saw Hank standing still, watching them, the frown on his face shouting his displeasure.

And Tonya knew, whatever she did, she'd better not wind up within her ex's grasp ever again.

Because this time he wouldn't just leave her for dead—he would finish the job.

TWO

Seth stirred, then pushed himself into a sitting position on the gurney and winced as his leg throbbed. Intense anger burned through him. Two months back on the circuit and he found himself injured again. This was not how he'd planned to spend his Thursday evening.

"Hey, hey, no sitting up." The paramedic on his left frowned at him. Seth ignored him but closed his eyes until the surge of dizziness passed. When his head stopped spinning, he opened his eyes and the EMT shrugged. "Okay, then, sit up. How do you feel?" The man bent over him, concern knitting his brow.

"Like I've been trampled by a bull." He waved a hand. "I'm fine." He gestured to his splinted leg. Someone had split the denim from hem to midthigh. "Is it broken?"

"Don't think so, just a very nasty bruise. You're fortunate you weren't hurt worse."

He grunted. "I'll give God—and Tonya—the credit." Fatigue swept over him. He turned his head and his gaze collided with a pair of sky blue eyes. Eyes that he'd not been able to get out of his head from their very first encounter. "Tonya? What are you doing here?"

The paramedic frowned. "You said to let her come."

"I did?" He didn't remember that…but *okay*. He lifted

a brow in her direction and was intrigued at the flush that darkened her cheeks. But what really caught his attention was the haunted skittishness in her eyes. He reached out and clasped her fingers in his. "I'm glad you're here."

The flush deepened. From the corner of his eye he saw the EMT relax a fraction. The blood-pressure cuff tightened on his arm. "Why did I pass out? Am I bleeding anywhere?"

"No, sir. Probably passed out from the pain."

"Right." He remembered the pain. Vividly. "That pain wasn't as bad as my break, though." Close, but not quite.

"That's a good thing."

"Which hospital are we heading for?"

"Vanderbilt University."

He nodded and leaned back, fighting the pain and the nausea. But he didn't let go of Tonya's hand. He liked the feel of her fingers in his. It helped him focus on something besides the throbbing in his leg.

When the ambulance pulled to a stop, he blinked the fog from his mind and tried to focus. They'd given him something for the pain and he felt groggy. Tonya's worried face kept going in and out of focus.

They wheeled him into the emergency department and he lost his grip on her hand. "Tonya?"

"I'm here." She slipped her hand back in his.

"Ma'am? You're going to have to wait in the waiting room."

"No." He didn't want her to leave, and while that shocked him, right now he didn't care. He tightened his grip. At least, he thought he did. "Stay. Let her stay."

They must have decided to listen to him. Tonya followed them back into the room.

She paced the floor, her gaze constantly going from a now-sleeping Seth to the small window in the door to check the hall. They'd rolled him to X-ray about thirty minutes after they'd been shown to the room and she'd been a nervous wreck until they'd returned. She slipped up to his side and covered his hand with hers. Even though he was pale and still, his strength was evident. She wanted to trace his square jaw and full lips. He had cheekbones a lot of women paid good money for. She allowed a faint smile to cross her lips. He had a good reputation in the bronc-busting world, and she had to admit every time he turned those smiling blue eyes in her direction, her knees went a little weak. She pushed a dark curl from his forehead and sighed when he didn't stir.

The nurse had explained Seth was on some powerful painkillers. "He'll be a bit loopy, dear," she'd said and checked his vitals one more time.

Tonya had nodded as she tried to decide what to do. She'd thought about slipping out of the hospital and disappearing, but where would she go? Home wasn't an option. Hank knew where she lived. He'd threatened her family once four years ago and she wouldn't give him the opportunity to do it again. She shuddered. It hadn't been proved, but she knew he'd been the one to run her youngest brother, Jacob, off the road and fire shots at his car. Jacob hadn't been hit, but Hank's point had been well made. No, she couldn't go home. She crossed her arms and moved to the small window once again.

Hank hadn't shown up at the hospital yet—as far as she knew—but that didn't mean he wouldn't. There were several possible hospitals in the city, but Vanderbilt was the best. He'd come here first. But surely he wouldn't get past security. Right? He might come in the same entrance as she and Seth, but that was as far as he would be able to get.

Unless he faked an illness or injury.

But he'd have to wait in the waiting room. They wouldn't bring him back immediately. She closed her eyes and dragged in a deep breath. She had to calm down. Stop her spinning thoughts.

"Tonya?"

She turned to find Seth watching her. "Hey. You're awake."

"You're still here."

She blinked. "I'm sorry… I can leave." But being in his room felt relatively safe. More safe than the outside world right now. And she realized she wasn't ready to leave, to give up the small measure of security she'd unexpectedly found in the hospital room.

"Leave? No, that's not what I meant. I'm just surprised you stayed."

"You asked me to."

"Oh. I did?"

She laughed. "Yes." Her laughter faded as quickly as it had bubbled up. She checked the window one more time.

"You should do that more often," he said gruffly.

"What?"

"Laugh."

Was he flirting? He'd just fallen off a bull and was laid up in the hospital—and he was flirting? She studied him with a small, uncertain smile. No. He was serious. She was almost disappointed.

She shook her head and, for the first time since entering the hospital, considered how she must look.

Clown paint on her face. Her hair tied up in a loose ponytail underneath the wig she still had on. Her cowboy hat dangled down her back. She had on a shirt that would rival one of Hawaii's brightest tucked into jeans that were covered with pink chaps. Cowboy boots finished the ensemble.

And the hospital staff hadn't blinked.

She started to respond to Seth, then saw his eyes were closed again and his chest rose and fell in a steady pattern. She sighed, pulled the bright red wig from her hair and dropped it on the chair. She went to the sink and grabbed several paper towels from the bin on the wall. She soaked them, added soap and did her best to get rid of the makeup.

When the door opened ten minutes later, Tonya felt halfway human again. The doctor entered. Tonya touched Seth's hand and gave him a gentle shake. "Seth?"

He stirred and opened his eyes. The doctor approached and Tonya moved toward the door. "I'll just wait outside."

"No," he murmured. "Stay. I might not remember a word he says."

Tonya caught the doctor's eye and he nodded. "All right."

She shut the door with one more glimpse out the window. She caught her breath and stared harder.

Was that Hank?

"Tonya?" She jerked and spun to find Seth's eyelids fluttering, his struggle against the desire to close them looking like a losing battle. "You okay?"

"Um…yes. I'm sorry. Someone caught my attention. I thought I might know him." She snapped her lips closed to quit jabbering.

The doctor held out a hand. "Dr. Jackson Mobley."

"Hi." Tonya shook his hand, her mind on the man she'd seen walk past the door. At Seth's curious look, she cleared her throat and tried to pay attention.

Dr. Mobley shook Seth's hand, then pushed the X-ray slides onto the machine and flipped the switch. Seth's leg popped up in black and white. The orthopedist pointed to an area with his pen. "Here's the former break. Nicely healed. The good news is that you didn't reinjure that. Nothing broken, just a bad bruise. I think you should pick back up on the physical therapy just to play it safe and you should be fine."

Seth leaned back, the relief on his face evident. "So I can ride tomorrow."

The doctor lifted his brow. "I don't recommend it. The muscles, tendons and ligaments are all bruised. You're very fortunate—I really expected to see you heading into surgery for something a lot more serious than this."

Seth sighed and rubbed a hand down his face. "I need to finish this rodeo. I had a good ride right before I fell off earlier. I'm in the running for the finals in December."

Dr. Mobley shrugged and gave a small smile. "I understand. I've followed your career and am a fan. I'd love to see you go to the National Finals Rodeo. We missed you last year after that bad break."

"But?" Seth nearly growled the word.

"But like I said, you can stay off of your leg for a couple of weeks and let it heal…or you can risk further injury."

Tonya eased toward the door one more time and glanced out. The workstation for the doctors and nurses was directly opposite. Everyone seemed busy. She glanced left, then right. No sign of Hank.

Wait. Was that him? She looked closer. The man talking to the nurse turned and she sucked in a deep breath. No doubt about it—that was *definitely* him. The shaggy hair and goatee couldn't hide his chillingly familiar features.

The doctor tapped her on the shoulder and she jumped with a high-pitched squeak. The man raised a brow and settled his hands on her upper arms. "Are you okay?"

Tonya felt the heat climb into her cheeks and nodded. "Sorry, I'm a bit jumpy today."

"No problem." He slipped out the door and she turned to find Seth appearing a little more alert.

"What are you looking for?"

"Nothing."

"Something. Or *someone*." Seth narrowed his eyes. "You've been looking out that window just about every other second—and you nearly just came out of your skin when the doc tapped your shoulder. What's going on, Tonya?" he asked, his voice lowered. "Is it the guy from earlier? The one you were hiding from in the supply room?"

"Yes." She twisted her hands together in front of her and debated how much she should say. What would he think if she told him the truth?

Then again, did she need to warn the hospital staff that a potential murderer had come through their doors? Hank wasn't predictable and he was here in the emergency department looking for her. Could everyone around her be in danger? "I'm pretty sure he's here at the hospital. It's been four years since I've seen him, but I think he was just talking to one of the nurses. I need to tell them to be on the alert and to warn security about the potential danger if he shows up."

She glanced through the window and, not seeing Hank, slipped out of the room before Seth could ask any more questions. She quietly told the nurse at the desk about Hank, waited for her to call security, then made her way back to Seth's room.

As she stepped inside, she heard a buzzing. One that she'd heard several times since arriving at the hospital. Seth noticed it, as well, and frowned. "What's that?"

Tonya pulled the buzzing phone from her back pocket

and held it out to him. "Jake tossed this to me when I got on the ambulance."

"That's my phone. He was holding it for me while I rode."

"You probably need to call him," she murmured. "It's been ringing for a while now."

Seth took it from her. "Okay, I'll call him in a few." He looked at the screen. "It's my mom." He pressed the button and lifted the phone to his ear. "Hello?" His eyes still hadn't left hers. "Yes, I'm fine. It's just a bruise." Tonya turned her back to give him the semblance of privacy even though she could hear every word. "No, Mom, you don't have to come to Nashville. It's not broken again, I promise. I'll call you later. Love you, too. 'Bye."

Tonya looked at him as he hung up. "She heard, I guess."

"Word travels fast. I've been doing rodeos for a long time. Some of the people have become like family. Extended family, anyway. One of the judges called Mom and Dad." Tonya nodded. "So who's the guy from the storage room? How do you know him?"

She sighed. "Earlier, at the arena, I went looking for Mia. She was getting her dogs ready, and as I was walking toward her, I recognized an old boyfriend." She glanced at the door.

"Old boyfriend, huh? Who?"

"Hank Newman."

"And why does his showing up make you skittish as a new colt?"

She crossed her arms. "A few years ago he tried to kill me."

Seth gaped at her. Then snapped his jaw shut. "Well, I guess that would do it."

"Indeed." His shock made her look away. This wasn't something she liked to talk about.

"Why?"

She forced her eyes back to his. "Why what?"

"Why would he try to kill you? That's insane."

Tonya huffed a short laugh. "Yes. Quite. We met my senior year of college. We had a couple of classes together. He asked me to marry him after three dates and I told him no. I'd already decided I didn't want to see him anymore and the marriage proposal sealed it. He asked me to reconsider. I wouldn't." She swallowed hard, then said, "This continued for the next several weeks. He'd show up at my apartment. If I refused to answer the door, he'd leave a gift."

"What kind of gift?"

She shrugged. "Flowers, chocolates, whatever he thought I might like. I finally had a restraining order taken out on him, but it didn't matter."

"Why? What happened?"

"He showed up at my apartment one day and caught me carrying groceries inside. I barely had a chance to shut the door before he kicked it in, furious and raving at me. He threw the restraining order in my face. I screamed at him to get out. He shouted he loved me." She'd shouted back that he didn't know what love was. "He finally calmed down a bit and tried reasoning with me. I got my phone out of my purse to call for help. He snatched it and threw it through a window. I raced for the door. He grabbed me, wrapped his hands around my throat and tried to strangle me."

She took a breath, let it out slowly. "I finally had the idea to just go limp right before I passed out. He must have let go immediately, thinking I was dead. One of my brothers, Grant, found me and got me to the hospital."

"And this psychopath is walking around free?"

Seth's outrage soothed some of her panic. "He went to jail but didn't stay there long. I've been hiding from him ever since. I have minimal contact with my family. I don't even want them knowing where I am." As she said the words aloud, an ache formed in her throat and tears rose to the surface. How she missed her big wonderful family. "I don't want them in danger. He threatened them once, almost killed Jacob, my youngest brother. I won't give him a reason to go after them again."

Seth held out a hand and she walked over to take it. His warm fingers wrapped around hers. "What are you going to do now that he's found you?"

"Run."

"You can't do that," Seth blurted out. His immediate desire to keep her close surprised him. Just like in the ambulance. He hadn't wanted her to leave then, and he didn't now. He frowned, wondering at the strangeness of his feelings. She lifted a brow and he waved a hand. "I mean, of course you *can*, but I don't want you to."

Tonya tilted her head and stared at him. "Well, what other choice do I have?"

"Fight him. Call the authorities. Tell them he's stalking you—harassing you—and you want it stopped."

She sighed, walked to the door to peer out one more time, then came back to sit on the edge of the bed. He drew in a deep breath, drinking in her scent. Vanilla, strawberries, something else. All mixed in with the smell of horses and leather. And possibly sweat and dirt. He loved it. She'd gotten most of the clown paint off her face, but she'd missed one spot on the side of her nose.

She looked down at her hands. "I wish it was that simple."

"Why isn't it?" He struggled back into a sitting position. His leg twinged, but the sharp tearing pain from earlier was gone.

She leaned over and helped adjust the pillow behind him. Her nearness nearly caused his heart to explode. Her tender care, her gentle touch, set his pulse to pounding.

He liked the way she did things almost without thinking. She'd noticed he could use a hand and offered one. He had to blink to focus on her words and resist the desire to pull her close.

"Because he's clever," she said. "No one ever sees him do anything wrong. In public he's in control, the nicest man you'd ever hope to meet. He could charm a bird out of a tree." She hesitated and he could see her fear escalating with whatever memories were going through her mind. "I've worked with the authorities before, to no avail. It took me almost dying to get him finally jailed." She shook her head. "I can't go through that again," she whispered.

He couldn't resist anymore. She'd offered him comfort just by being there with him. He grasped her upper arm and pulled her close. She tensed and he stopped, wondering if he was being too forward. Then something seemed to snap inside of her and she leaned into him, wrapped her arms around him and rested her head against his shoulder.

He held her and she let him. "I haven't said thank you."

She pulled away and he wished he'd kept his big mouth shut. She sniffed and grabbed a tissue from the box near his bed. "For what?"

"You saved my life today and I haven't even thanked you."

"Oh. You're welcome."

He laughed. "You say that like it's no big deal."

Tonya flushed. "Of course your life is a big deal."

"I didn't mean that. I meant you act like what you do, the risks you take, is not a big thing. It's crazy and admirable and dangerous."

She shrugged. "I don't think about the danger so much. I mean, I know I could be seriously hurt one day, or even killed, but I'm good at what I do and I'm careful." She paused and tilted her head. "And I pray a lot."

"I know you're careful. I've seen you work, Ms. Rodeo Clown of the Year."

She flushed again. "Stop."

"It's impressive. You want to get to the NFR this year, too, as one of the barrelmen, don't you?"

"Of course I do, but you know as well as I do that's a long shot. I work in a man's world where the good-ol'-boy system is alive and well." He knew what she meant. Peers voted for whom they thought deserved to go to the NFR and work in the arena. Only three went. And the men tended to stick together when it came down to the voting.

The knock on the door startled them both. Tonya stood as the doctor walked in. "All right, Mr. Starke, you're good to go. The nurse will be by with your papers shortly. Are you allergic to anything?"

Seth shot the orthopedist a sour look. "You mean besides the apparent newly acquired allergy of bull riding?"

Dr. Mobley smiled. "Yes."

"Then that would be a no."

"Excellent. I've prescribed you some painkillers in case you need them. You'll probably be able to walk, but it won't be comfortable. We'll get you a wheelchair to get you out of here."

Seth scowled. "No wheelchair. I'll be fine. The fact that I can walk is better than any drug you've got."

"All right, then. All the best to you."

"Thanks."

The nurse entered shortly after Dr. Mobley left. Seth signed the papers. "Do you need anything for pain before you go?"

Seth gave his leg a test move and stood. He gasped and gritted his teeth but was able to stay upright and keep the weight on it. Mostly. Relief pushed aside the pain. "No, the other drugs are just starting to wear off. I don't need anything else right now."

The nurse nodded, pulled her copies from the stack and handed Seth the others. "Take care of yourself."

"Right."

She looked at Tonya. "We haven't seen the man you told us about. I think he may have left."

"Good."

Seth turned toward her. Tonya's face was pale and frightened, but she lifted her chin up a notch. "Are you sure you're all right?" he asked.

She drew in a deep breath. "I will be." He took a step and hissed at the lightning that shot through his thigh. "What about you?" she asked.

"It hurts, but I'll make it."

Tonya stepped up beside him and wrapped an arm around his waist. "Lean on me if you need to."

Her offer melted something inside him. When was the last time—discounting his family—someone had genuinely wanted to do something for him?

Just because. Not as an expectation that he would do something in return. He couldn't remember. "I'd squash you." But he wasn't going to argue about the close proximity. Quite frankly, he relished it.

She frowned. "I'm stronger than I look."

He settled her under his shoulder and took another deep breath. "All right, let's go."

"Just one thing."

"What's that?" he asked, looking down at her up-turned face.

"I want to go out the back. I know I saw Hank here and I know he's waiting on me to walk out the way we came in."

THREE

Her heart trembled when Seth nodded and, without another word, led her toward the back exit. His limp was pronounced, but at least he was on his feet. She kept her head tilted toward him but her eyes bounced off each face she passed.

They exited the back of the ER into another part of the hospital. "Did you see him?" Seth asked.

"No." But it didn't mean he wasn't watching. Just waiting for her to step outside the hospital, where she would be an easy mark. "He was in the emergency department," she said. "I know it was him."

"How do you think he got back there?"

"I told you. He's charming."

"How did he even know you were here?"

She swallowed and paused. Seth stopped and leaned against the wall to take the weight off his sore leg. Tonya noticed his ruggedly tanned cheeks were about two shades lighter than normal. "Hank saw me get in the ambulance. I spotted him and that's why I wanted to hitch a ride with you." She bit her lip. "I'm sorry."

Realization dawned. "Ah. So all he had to do was call around and ask if I was in the ED. Pretend he was my brother or something and was looking for me."

"Or simply follow the ambulance if his car was nearby."

His lips quirked up in a half smile. "So, you weren't so concerned about me—you were just trying to get away from him."

Stricken, she grasped his hand. "Of course I was concerned—"

He placed a finger over her lips. "I'm just teasing, Tonya. I'm glad you hitched the ride with me. To tell you the truth, it was good to have you there." She saw his Adam's apple bob. "I didn't feel so alone."

Tonya blew out an unsteady breath and glanced back over her shoulder as his words resonated within her. She had been concerned, downright *terrified* for him. She closed her eyes and willed her heart to slow its racing beat. *Don't be attracted to him. Don't even think about it. Haven't you learned your lesson with Daniel?* The harsh mental reprimand didn't slow her heart rate, but the memory of Daniel's death allowed her to put some emotional distance between her and Seth. She took a step and glanced over at him. "I think we should go."

"How? We don't have a car."

"That's why God invented cabs. Or we can call Jake. He offered to clean out his truck for you."

Seth wrinkled his nose. "No way. I'll take the cab." They started walking again—or rather, she walked while Seth limped along beside her. Tonya's gaze bounced off each person within eyesight. She finally drew in a steady breath and decided maybe Hank had given up and left. She didn't fool herself into thinking it was a permanent absence, but as long as she could get Seth home safe, that was all that mattered right now.

She pulled out her phone and looked up the number for the cab company. Seth shifted and a low grunt escaped him. "You should have taken that offer of the wheel-chair," she murmured.

He shot her an insulted look. "Not this buckaroo."

Tonya rolled her eyes, then tapped the number that popped up onto her screen. Within seconds she had a cab on the way. "I'm going back to my RV and pulling out," she said softly.

"Where are you going to go? What about your job?"

She groaned. He had a good point. As of today, her reputation on the circuit was stellar. If she left now, her name in the industry would suffer. Was she willing to let Hank do that? He'd already taken away just about everything she cared about. Was she going to let him take this, too?

She lifted her chin. Seth was right—she had to finish the show. Then she could disappear. "Okay, then. As soon as the rodeo's over, I'll leave." And cancel her other obligations until it was safe to surface again. She bit her lip as they continued their slow progress toward the lobby, where the cab would pick them up. "I can cancel the contest I was going to compete in next weekend."

"You're winning quite a few of those, aren't you?"

She shrugged and smiled. "It's a way to earn some extra money and I like them. The element of danger isn't quite so nerve-racking." Her smile slipped back into a frown. "But what am I going to do about Hank? What if he shows up at the rodeo tomorrow?"

"When we get back, we'll move your motor home to another spot on the grounds. We'll talk to rodeo security, make sure they're keeping an eye on your place. We'll also be up-front and honest about the fact that you have a stalker."

They reached the lobby of the hospital and Tonya kept

her back against one of the walls while she watched for the cab to pull up in the circular area.

When it did, she slipped an arm around Seth's waist. He allowed her to help support him without a word. Which said a lot to her about his pain level. And stubbornness. His breath warmed her ear, threatening to shatter her composure.

With a steadying breath, and a refusal to acknowledge her rapid pulse, she helped him into the backseat of the cab then went around to the other side to get in behind the driver.

"You're strong," Seth said.

"I have to be." He knew that, but she could see it still surprised him. She turned in the seat to look out the back window. No sign of Hank. But she knew that could be deceptive. She'd thought he was gone from her life at one time and he'd shown back up with a vengeance. Fear shivered through her. What was she going to do? The thought of facing him down terrified her. *Lord, show me what to do.*

She gave the driver the address for the rodeo grounds. Seth leaned his head back and closed his eyes. Tonya started to reach for his hand and stopped. She couldn't let herself care for him any more. She couldn't develop any feelings for him. Or depend on him. Not just because she was leaving, but because he could break her heart.

But she silently admitted she'd always liked Seth, thought he was one of the cowboys who just had a special quality about him. She'd heard the rumors, of course, about his girlfriend leaving him after he broke his leg. That he'd been devastated but more determined than ever to make a comeback.

And he had. He held the fifteenth spot and she had no doubt he would continue to move up the list as he kept winning rodeos. He would be riding the NFR and she wouldn't be around to see it. The thought made her inexplicably sad.

Exhaustion swamped her, but she still had a long night ahead of her. She glanced at her phone. Mia had called four times. She called her friend back.

"Are you okay?" Mia demanded. "Where are you?"

"I'm fine. I went to the hospital with Seth."

"That was some crazy move you did over that fence."

A small smile curled her lips. She felt relieved she had a reason to actually smile about something. "I suppose I should thank my parents for all of the gymnastics classes in my youth."

"Is there anything you need?" Mia's voice had lost its edge, softening now that her worry was eased. She could picture her best friend's forehead creased with worry. Mia's tall, lanky build disguised her ability to move with speed when faced with an angry bull. Her friend's agility in the arena was amazing and she had fans who came from all over to watch her perform.

"No, I'm on the way back with Seth. The bull bruised Seth's leg, but we're grateful it wasn't broken again." She paused. "Mia?"

"Yeah?"

"You know that man I told you about? Hank Newman?"

"Hank Newman? No… Wait. The guy who tried to kill you in college? The one you said stalked you?"

"Yes."

"What about him?"

"He was there today. At the rodeo."

"*What?* Are you sure?" Mia's skepticism came through loud and clear.

"I'm sure."

"But…why?"

"I think we know why."

"Did you call the police?"

Tonya sighed. "No. Not yet. I haven't had the chance. But, I mean, what's the point in calling them, anyway? If past experience is anything to go by, it's not like they can do anything. All he's done is come to a rodeo. That's not against the law."

"Surely the fact that he tried to kill you before would hold some weight in what they could do, wouldn't it?"

Tonya thought about that. She was still so shaken that Hank had found her, she wasn't thinking straight. "I don't know. Maybe. I'll have to find out."

"I think you really should. Be careful, Tonya. You never know what he might do." She paused. "Actually, you do know what he might do. Best to avoid that."

She hung up with her friend and closed her eyes.

"You okay?" Seth asked.

"I'm scared," she admitted without opening her eyes. "I can do high-wire acts, let someone springboard me out of a cannon and face down ornery bulls, but the thought of coming face-to-face with Hank Newman paralyzes me with a fear I don't know what to do with."

She felt his hand close around hers with a gentleness that disguised his strength. The instant comfort she felt surprised her—warmed her. "We'll go to the police if you see him again."

"At first I didn't think going to the police would even matter. But Mia pointed out the fact that he has been jailed for trying to kill me, so maybe…"

"We'll get a restraining order."

She sighed. "Like I already told you, I've done that before. And I'll do it again, of course, but he doesn't care. It didn't stop him from tracking me down at work the day he got out of prison, and I'm afraid it won't stop him now."

"My brother is a sheriff's deputy in Wrangler's Corner. I'll ask his advice."

"Okay. Thanks." She'd let him do that but didn't hold out much hope that it would help. After all, she'd already been down that road once before. She knew it led only to a dead end.

Seth's leg burned with an ache that kept him tossing and turning, trying to find a comfortable position on the mattress. He finally threw the sheets off and sat up. *1:40 a.m.* He sighed and debated about taking a pain pill. He hadn't bothered filling the prescription the doctor had given him earlier, but he had a few left from his first fall.

If he was honest, it wasn't really his leg that was bothering him as much as it was what he'd learned tonight about Tonya Waters. Someone had tried to kill her—and apparently that someone was back. He shook his head. There were some crazy people out there.

During the cab ride back to the rodeo grounds, he'd gathered his strength and called Jake, whose trailer was right next to Seth's. After Seth explained the situation, his buddy had agreed to swap sites with Tonya.

"That's way too much trouble," Tonya had protested.

"What if I need something during the night? What if something happens and I need you to come help me out?"

She'd narrowed her eyes, clearly not buying it and knowing as well as he did that Jake would be there for him if he needed it. But she'd sighed and shrugged. "Okay, you win."

"It's not about winning, Tonya—it's about making sure you're safe. And besides, security is close by, as well as some of the other bull riders. If anything happens, you'll have help."

She'd bitten her lip and nodded. Then fought the tears he'd seen gathering in her pretty blue eyes. "All right. I'm not going to be stupid. Thank you."

The process had taken a grand total of thirty minutes. One thing about living on the road: buckaroos and bull-fighters had the art of moving down to a science.

Now Tonya was tucked in her motor home next to his.

And he still couldn't sleep.

He walked into the kitchen to grab a cup of water. Standing at the window, he studied Tonya's motor home. She had one she drove—a Class C. Seth looked around his fifth wheel. Space-wise, his was larger, roomier than Tonya's, but he had to haul his behind his truck. But he didn't mind. When he wasn't on the circuit, he was home in Wrangler's Corner, his fifth wheel parked in a space on the property where he could hook up and have his own privacy. One day he'd build a house there.

A house for his wife, his family.

He couldn't help glancing at Tonya's motor home one more time. The light was still on, the brightness peeking around the edges of her pulled curtains.

He'd heard the rumors, of course. That after Daniel's death, she'd closed herself off from any romantic entanglements with those in the business. He sighed. He understood it. He felt the same way. After Glory's betrayal, he'd vowed that he'd make sure a woman loved him for himself, not his name or the money in his savings account. He grimaced and massaged the muscles above the bruise on his sore leg. Why was he even pondering these things? He was being silly.

No. He was lonely. He wanted a wife, a marriage. One like his parents'. They'd been married thirty-seven years. They'd had good times and bad, but they'd stuck it out and stayed together. Which was exactly what he was looking for.

Too bad the women he seemed to be attracted to didn't feel the same way. Except maybe Tonya.

"Enough." He swallowed the last of the water in his glass and headed back to bed. If he was going to ride tomorrow, he needed to sleep.

Tonya jerked awake, heart pounding, blood rushing. She shoved into a sitting position on the couch where she'd dozed off and rubbed a hand down her face. She hadn't meant to fall asleep. She couldn't sleep until she was in a safe place. Right now Hank knew where she was. He might have to hunt a little to find her motor home, but she had no doubt he'd find her. She'd just bought herself a little time with the move. But how much time?

Tonya got up and grabbed her laptop. She opened the lid and powered her phone on to use as a hot spot for the internet.

Once she had her search engine up, she typed in *Hank Newman*. Several options came up. The newspaper article detailing his arrest record, the police report, the restraining order. Nothing she didn't already know.

Next she typed in *Tonya Lewis*. Her birth name. The name she hadn't used in over four years. She'd thought she'd be safe. Her major in college had been agriculture. Once she'd finished school, she'd gone to work for a business and had an office job.

And Hank had found her. Through the cracked blinds of her office, she'd happened to look up and see him walk in to speak to the receptionist. Tonya's heart had dropped to her toes when the woman had pointed straight at her office. Tonya'd grabbed her purse and her personal laptop and escaped through the back door. She'd never gone back.

And during the course of their three dates, she'd never shared her passion for bullfighting with Hank. Which was why she'd thought she could hide out on the circuit.

And it had worked till now.

A creak at the back of the motor home swung her attention to the bedroom. She could see straight back, so she knew someone wasn't inside. It was just the wind blowing. Clouds had darkened the sky before the sun had set and a storm was predicted for early morning. But she couldn't help that her nerves jumped at every sound. She knew they would until she got out of Nashville.

But where would she go? What would she do now that her very livelihood had been threatened? This was her job, her life now. She couldn't go back to an office.

Another scraping noise set her heart pounding. Again the sound came from the back. But that wasn't the wind. She'd pulled the coverings over the windows at the front and the back. No one could see in, but she couldn't see out either.

Tonya moved, her legs shaking. She tested the lock on the door. Secure. The door opened outward. No one could kick it in, so no one was coming in that way. Her breathing quickened.

A sound at the window over the couch made her spin around. In a flash, she knew what was going on. Someone was going window to window trying them. Seeing if he could find one unlocked. The windows slid left to right and had a flimsy screen over them. Easily removed.

And the windows were large. Someone could climb right in if he got one open. She waited, listening, trying to discern where he was. A thump overhead? A footstep?

Should she get out of the motor home? Cause a ruckus

so people would come investigate? She crept toward the door. The handle rattled, sending every nerve in her body skittering with fear. She jerked her hand away and grabbed her cell phone. Shaky fingers punched in 911. Her breath came in low pants. The knob rattled again. Then footsteps leaving. She bit her lip.

"What's your emergency?"

"Someone's trying to break in my motor home. I'm at the rodeo fairgrounds arena." She gave the address and prayed the woman could hear her. "He rattled my doorknob and tried my windows. I heard his footsteps leaving, but I don't know if he's gone or just trying to figure out another way to get in."

The loud crash at the back of the motor home startled her into fumbling the phone. She dropped to her knees next to the device, her clumsy fingers grasping for it.

She looked up to see a man step out of her bathroom. He rushed toward her and for a moment she froze, paralyzed with fear. Then she spun for the door. Dropped the phone but got her fingers around the knob.

The sickeningly sweet odor of his familiar cologne took her back to the day she almost died. She twisted the lock.

Felt a hand in her hair and he yanked her back.

Tonya screamed.

FOUR

Seth slammed the door of his fifth wheel shut behind him. He started to sit on the top step when the scream that came from Tonya's motor home froze him for a split second. Then he snapped into action. He ignored the arching pain in his leg and raced across the short strip of red dirt to pound on her door. He tried the knob and found it locked. "Tonya! Open the door!"

A loud crash came from within. Seth stood on the second step, gripped the railing on either side for balance, leaned back and gave the door a swift kick with his good leg. It shuddered but didn't even come close to opening. "Tonya!"

Lights in nearby motor homes flipped on. "What's going on out there?" someone called.

"Call the police!" Seth shouted.

The door flew open, catching Seth in the shoulder. He moved back slightly and caught a glimpse of Tonya's terrified face. A man in a ski mask tried to reach out to grab the door to close it, but Seth was faster. He bypassed the door and snatched the man's wrist. He yanked and the masked intruder stumbled forward, out the door and down the steps. Seth shot out a fist. The man ducked and kicked, grazing Seth's injured leg. Seth lost his balance and went down with a grunt. He rolled and stuck out a hand to snag the man's leg. And missed. Sirens sounded in the distance.

Seth managed to get to his feet. Sleepy residents were moving slow, not realizing what was happening yet. But some of the other bull riders Seth had alerted to the fact that there might be danger were moving fast. The man in the ski mask fled. Two of the bull riders went after him.

Seth gritted his teeth against the renewed throbbing in his leg and lifted his head to find Tonya headed toward him, tears streaming down her cheeks.

Bruises had already started to form on her throat and rage ignited within him as Seth deduced what had happened. The man had broken into her motor home with the intention of killing her.

Just as he'd tried to do four years ago.

Seth reached for her and she stumbled into his arms to collapse against his chest. He wrapped his arms around her, balancing himself and her on his good leg and taking his weight off the one that screamed at him. "Shh," he whispered against her ear. "It's all right. He's gone."

She clung to him fiercely, her shoulders shaking, not making a sound. But he could feel the warmth of her tears soaking through his shirt. He held her close, trying to offer her the comfort and safety she so desperately needed. Officers descended. Security and rodeo personnel arrived. Seth drew in a deep breath, the scent of her strawberry shampoo mingling with sweat and fear making him tighten his grip.

She finally stirred and brushed a hand across her wet cheeks. "Are you all right? Your leg?" she whispered.

His heart stuttered. She was concerned about him when she'd been almost killed? He simply nodded. "I'm fine."

"Ma'am, can you tell me what happened?"

Using the palms of her hands, she scrubbed the rest of the tears from her cheeks. Seth rested his hand on her shoulder, just to remind her that she wasn't alone.

Her jaw tightened and her eyes narrowed. She seemed to shrug off her fear, but Seth could still feel the fine tremor beneath his palm. "I can tell you exactly what happened," she rasped, then cleared her throat. "I heard a noise, like someone checking to see if any of my windows were unlocked. They weren't. I decided to call 911 when I heard someone on the roof. He came through the overhead bathroom vent." She spread her hands and shook her head. "Just crashed through and came out the door and…there he was." A shudder ran through her. "I tried to get to the door and he grabbed me." She touched her bruised throat.

"Did you recognize your attacker?" the policeman asked.

"He had on a mask, but I know it was Hank Newman."

The officer lifted a brow. "How do you know that if he had on a mask?"

"Because I recognized his cologne. And—" she drew in a deep, cleansing breath "—it's not the first time he's tried to kill me."

"Oh." The policeman frowned and wrote something in his little notebook. "All right. Anything else?"

She looked at Seth. "When you pounded on the door, it startled him. He loosened his grip enough for me to get away and get the door open. Thank you for that," she whispered.

"Hey, I owed you. You saved me from a trampling today." He gave her a gentle smile. Her tension lessened by a fraction. She smiled back but it was shaky and tight.

"I just wish I could have kept him from getting away," Seth muttered. His leg was on fire, but not so intensely he was unable to ignore it. For now. Tomorrow would be worse, he knew.

An EMT approached. "Ma'am, would you like us to take a look at you?"

She shook her head. "I've been through this before. There's nothing you can do for a bruised throat."

Seth finished telling his side of the story and the officers left, armed with Hank Newman's photo, but Seth knew they didn't have enough evidence to arrest the man. He'd had a mask on. Tonya might believe it was Hank, but without solid proof, the creep would continue to be free to terrorize her.

Unless Seth did something to protect her. He mulled that thought over while friends and fellow roadies hugged Tonya and told her they were there for her.

"Tonya! Tonya! Where are you?"

Tonya spun to find herself engulfed in Mia's slender arms. She winced at the tight hug, her new bruises protesting, but she didn't pull away. Her best friend finally let her go and stepped back to give her the once-over. "Are you all right? I just heard someone broke into your motor home." Her eyes landed on Tonya's throat and widened. "What did he do?"

"Tried to strangle me. Again."

"Again?"

"Yes."

"So you were right. He *was* here."

"*Is* here. I saw him earlier on the grounds and at the hospital. I have no doubt it was him in my home." She swallowed hard. "He's back and apparently he wants to see me dead."

Mia paled. "What are you going to do? You still have

a show to do tomorrow. Not to mention the contest in a couple of weeks."

"Don't worry—I'm not going to leave you in the lurch."

"Are you kidding? Your life is more important than some stupid show. I can handle it. And there are always other contests out there. You just do whatever you need to do."

Tonya's heart gave a grateful beat. "Thanks, Mia, but I think I'll be all right. Hank is probably long gone by now."

A slight pause. Mia eyed her. "You don't really believe that, do you?"

Tonya sighed. "No, not really, but I refuse to let that loser send me running again. I'm not going to let him ruin my reputation in this business. I've worked hard to get where I am." Even though the thought of standing her ground and fighting back terrified her.

"But—"

"But nothing. I'm staying." Saying the words made it so for her.

"Okay, okay."

Tonya pulled in a deep breath. "Sorry, I didn't mean to snap."

"No, it's fine. Let me know if you need me to do anything. You want to come stay with me?"

Tonya considered that. "What about Monty?"

"I'll kick him out. He can bunk with Jake or one of the other guys." When Tonya still hesitated, Mia rolled her eyes. "Come on. You know my brother won't care."

"All right. If he says it's okay, I'll stay with you. Thanks. I'll have to get something to cover up the hole in my roof and then I'll get someone to walk me over."

"Great. I'll go get your bed ready."

"Thanks, Mia."

"Of course." Tonya watched her friend walk away, still in shock over the events that had transpired. Fortunately, Mia's fifth wheel was only a few rows over.

"I have some tarp I can put over the hole until you can get someone out here to fix it," Seth said.

"Thank you." She bit her lip and let her eyes linger on his handsome face. He really was a good guy.

"I'll walk you over to Mia's and then come back and do it."

She frowned. "I can help you."

"No need. Won't take but a few minutes. You need to rest."

"What about your leg?"

"It hurts, but it won't keep me from doing what needs to be done." He nodded at her motor home. "Get what you need for the night. I'll take care of the rest."

Tonya struggled with the notion. She wasn't the kind of female who needed a man to take over or take care of her. She'd grown up with that for the first two decades of her life with four older brothers. Part of her wanted to rebel and assert her independence, but Seth didn't come across as doing it because he thought she couldn't. He genuinely seemed to want to do it because it would be helping her, *not* controlling her. She'd learned how to discern between the two. Finally, she gave a slow nod. "Okay. Thank you."

"I'll go get the tarp and be right back."

She watched him go. Then turned back to face the steps that would take her into her home. Where she'd just been attacked. She swallowed a lump in her throat. She didn't want to go inside. Not by herself. A hand fell on her shoulder. She jumped and screamed.

"Hey, it's me. I'm sorry."

Seth. Tonya slapped a hand over her thudding heart-beat. "You scared me to death."

"I'm sorry. I called your name twice."

"Oh. Didn't expect you back so soon." She twisted her hands in front of her. "I was just going in to pack."

"And you don't want to go inside alone."

She flushed, surprised he read her so well. Then again, she hadn't realized he'd been watching her either. "Not really."

"Come on." He took her hand and led the way up the steps and into the motor home. She gave his fingers a squeeze and blinked at the mess.

"Wow."

"Wow is right," he echoed. "You really put up a fight."

"Yeah." She stepped over the ottoman and the pillows from the couch that had somehow wound up on the floor. "I'll be just a minute."

"No problem."

She stopped at the bathroom and peeked inside. Plastic and glass littered the area. The fan hung by a short wire from the ceiling. She sighed and gathered her toiletries and shut the door.

Ten minutes later, she had a packed bag. She walked back into the living area to find everything put back in its place. "Thank you."

"You're welcome."

"I'm saying that a lot, aren't I?"

He winked at her. "Hey, you saved my life. I owe you."

"Stop saying that. I did my job." He frowned and she rubbed her eyes. "That didn't come out right."

"I understand. Come on. I'll walk you over to Mia's. I have a friend in the area who owns an RV shop. I'll call him and see how fast he can get you fixed up."

"That would be amazing."

He smiled and her heart flipped. She froze. No, no, no, no. She couldn't be attracted to him. She couldn't. She'd sworn off buckaroos. She'd vowed never to get involved with someone in the rodeo ever again. And what was her traitorous heart doing? Going all crazy over Seth Starke. A buckaroo. Just like Daniel had been. It was just a reaction to the stress, to finding comfort in his arms, to... something. Anything but that she was truly drawn to him.

She cleared her throat and stepped toward the door. Confusion flickered in his blue eyes, but he didn't say anything, just followed her outside.

As she walked away from her home, she couldn't help the shudder that raced up her spine. Was her ex truly gone? Or was he in the shadows, hiding behind one of the RVs in the crowded park?

Seth slid an arm across her shoulders and she left it there, appreciating his nearness, the comfort his strong, steady presence offered. She *did* appreciate it even though she might not *want* to appreciate it.

Mia opened the door to her trailer as they approached. Her eyes widened slightly at the sight of Seth's arm around Tonya's shoulders. Tonya moved away from him. She didn't want to give Mia the wrong idea.

"Come on in," her friend said. "I've got the top bunk all made up for you."

"Thanks, Mia."

She nodded, paused and gave Tonya and Seth another lingering look. Knowing what her girlfriend must be thinking, Tonya lifted a brow and Mia flushed. "I'm just going to go get the dogs' leashes. Now that they're up, they'll want to go out for the night."

"Thanks, Mia." Once her friend disappeared into her trailer, Tonya gazed up at Seth. "Thank you for everything. Again."

"Of course." He cleared his throat. "I know the police here are working on it, but as I mentioned before, my brother Clay is a sheriff's deputy in my hometown. Would you mind if I gave him a call and filled him in on everything that happened tonight? He could do some looking into Mr. Newman's background and see if he's got an address or what the latest is on him. He might even find out something before these guys do."

"Sure, that would be great."

"I'll see you tomorrow, then."

Tonya looked around, probing the darkness, feeling the dread of spending the next few hours in the dark settle in the pit of her stomach. But she'd be with Mia. It would be all right.

Wouldn't it?

FIVE

Friday morning dawned hot and humid. Tonya stood at the window of Mia's little kitchen, looking out over the area. Trailers, motor homes, RVs and fifth wheels filled all the slots. She breathed in the smell of bacon and coffee. Coffee. Her one vice. Okay, one of two vices. She seemed to have a thing for bull riders, too. Her lips twisted. While she loved coffee and drank a lot of it, she needed to avoid the buckaroos. Especially a tall, good-looking, blue-eyed bull rider.

She moved to the table and shoved aside the deck of cards and poker chips. She shook her head and frowned.

She sipped on her second cup and thought about her life. *God, I believe You're in control and nothing is happening to me that You don't allow. But this is a hard one.* Hank Newman. Just thinking his name sent shivers up her spine. And not the good kind. Not the kind being around Seth Starke elicited.

"You ready?"

Tonya gave a little start and lifted her head at Mia's voice. Her friend was already up and dressed, her dogs prancing near their leashes hanging on a peg next to the door. "I'm ready." She gestured to the cards and chips. "I didn't realize you were into gambling."

Mia hesitated a moment, then shrugged. "Not me. Monty. He plays with some of the guys occasionally."

"I appreciate him bunking with someone else so I could stay here last night." There was barely room for two people, much less three.

"Of course. He probably preferred it." She gave a small smile. "He says I nag him too much."

"Who? You? You're kidding." Tonya let the teasing sarcasm slip into her tone and Mia gave a short laugh.

"I know, right? I can't help it. I'm his big sister. I'm supposed to take care of him." She frowned and took a deep breath. "These days I just can't seem to do a very good job with that."

"Monty's a grown man. He can take care of himself."

"Yeah." She waved a hand to dismiss the subject. "Now...*he's* not going to mess with your concentration, is he?"

Who? Seth or Hank? "No. I refuse to let him." The answer fit for either man.

"Have you decided what you're going to do about that creep, Hank?"

"No, I'm still thinking."

"Okay, well, while you're thinking, I'm going to get the day started." Mia hooked the dogs' leashes on, grabbed her scooper and a plastic bag and opened the door. "We'll be back."

"I'll be getting ready."

Mia left, leaving Tonya alone with her thoughts once more. And those thoughts kept leading her to Seth. In a way he reminded her of her brothers. Strong, caring, protective. She grimaced at the last word but had been grateful for that particular trait last night.

Tonya dressed for the day, still trying to decide what to do, where she would go. She had one more show to do;

then she could either take some time off and go into hiding for a while, or she could take her chances and fight back. For a moment she considered calling her family. Her brothers would drop everything and rush to her side. But then she remembered Hank's threats. "All it takes is one bullet," he'd hissed. "And I've got plenty of those."

Mia came back and let the dogs inside. Shaggy, the white-and-brown terrier mix, leaped up onto the couch and settled himself on the end. Scrappie, a larger golden retriever, gave Tonya's hand a wet kiss. She scratched his ears and smiled. Animals were such innocent and sweet creatures. She had to admit it would be nice to have your every need catered to. And to not have to worry if someone was trying to kill you.

Or if they'd eventually succeed.

"You all right?" Mia asked as she hung the leashes on their hooks.

"I'm hanging in there." Tonya forced a smile.

"We have about an hour before we have to be at the arena. Did you eat?"

"A granola bar. I'm not hungry. I think I'm going to go ahead and go over there. I want to check my barrel and get into costume in the dressing room." *And avoid thinking about last night.*

Mia frowned. "All right, let me grab my bag and we'll go together. You probably don't need to be walking alone."

Tonya hadn't planned on it. She'd already decided to ask Seth if he'd walk with her. But maybe it was better this way. She'd already spent entirely too much time thinking about the handsome buckaroo. Not just in the past twenty-four hours but over the past year since Daniel's death. Seth had been one of the first ones to offer his condolences in the face of his own grief over losing one of his best friends…and she hadn't forgotten that. Only now her feelings had started to turn from friendship to more of an attraction. A romantic interest.

The very idea scared her to death. She gathered her bag and scolded herself for her thoughts. There was no way she would put herself through that again. She refused to love someone who rode a bull for a living. Her heart had only just healed from losing Daniel. And while the grief had faded some, the guilt hadn't.

And besides, Seth was still nursing his own wounded heart. Tonya knew Glory had dumped Seth soon after he'd broken his leg. He hadn't even been discharged from the hospital and she'd already written him off and walked out. Tonya had never cared much for the woman, but after that incident, she avoided being around her as much as possible.

"I'm ready when you are," Mia said. "Come on. We'll take the golf cart. I don't feel like walking. It was a late night."

The arena was about a mile and a half away. Tonya wouldn't have minded the hike but didn't argue. She followed Mia out the door and down the steps to the golf cart. The dogs hopped onto the back and Tonya climbed in beside Mia.

"You have room for one more?"

Tonya's stomach knotted and she turned in the seat to find Seth walking toward them. "Sure, hop on." Freshly shaven and dressed to ride, he looked as attractive as ever. She also noted that he walked with a slight limp. "How's the leg?"

"Not great, but not as bad as I'd thought it was going to be." He grimaced and settled himself beside Tonya. She gulped at his nearness. His broad shoulder rested against hers and she tried to scoot a bit toward Mia.

Mia gunned the gas and they headed for the arena. Others were up and on the way, as well. They merged with the crowd. Tonya couldn't help examining everyone she could see. Was Hank lurking around? Was he looking for her even now? She drew in a deep breath and focused on the man beside her. "Are you going to be able to ride?" she asked him.

"I don't really have a choice if I hope to keep my spot in the finals."

Tonya tensed. "If your leg isn't strong enough, you won't be able to hold on. You could fall again."

"Yeah. I know."

She knew he knew. They all knew. Including the crowd surging into the arena just ahead. Seth's fall and subsequent injury had been big news in the rodeo industry yesterday. The fact that he planned to ride today was even bigger. Rodeo fans would make a special effort to come out and cheer him on. Or root for his failure, depending on who their favorite was. Tonya clamped her lips shut and tried to mentally prepare herself for the next bullfight.

"Hey, Mia, I never got my rope back from yesterday. Did you pick it up?"

"Yes, it's in the storage room. I hung it on the wall."

"Thanks."

After every bull ride, the rodeo clowns usually were the ones who gave the rope back to the buckaroo. In Seth's case, since he'd been injured and on the way to the hospital, storing it was the only option until he could claim it. She noticed his frown. "What is it?"

"I keep going over the fall from yesterday. Something wasn't right."

"Exactly. You fell."

"No," he said and shot her a twisted smile. "That's

not what I mean. It was right before I was going to dismount from the bull. The rope slipped—or something."

Mia scoffed. "How would that happen? You put that rope on yourself."

"I know, but I think I remember it moving and that's what threw me off balance."

Tonya studied his serious features. Seth was a really good-looking man. And he had a kind heart to round out the whole appealing package. "Seth, you've been putting ropes on bulls for a long time. Have you ever had one slip before?"

"Never. Which is why I want to take a look at it." He gestured toward the bag at his feet. "I have another one for today but want to check out the one from yesterday."

Mia parked the golf cart and pocketed the key. They flashed their badges, made their way into the arena and headed to the area where they would get ready for the show.

Seth stopped Tonya with a hand on her arm. Mia kept going into the dressing room. "Are you sure you're up to this? We're both pretty beat up from yesterday. I don't want you to worry about me."

Tonya stared at him. She was in exactly the position she didn't want to be in. He was starting to care about her. Yesterday when he offered her comfort and security, she hadn't been thinking about this moment. A moment very similar to the one that had gotten Daniel killed because he'd been distracted by his feelings for her. "I'm fine." She forced a coldness into her voice. "You do your job and just let me do mine. Don't let your emotions or worry for me cloud your judgment."

He blinked. Then withdrew his hand from her arm. She felt his emotional withdrawal, as well, and wanted to blurt out that she didn't mean it, that she was sorry.

Instead she bit her lip. It was for his own good. He gave her a short nod. "See you."

"Seth—"

He raised a hand. "I'll see you."

Regret washed over her. "All right."

He walked away and she shook off the wish that she'd handled that differently. She felt so alone. Truly alone. A shiver danced up her spine and she looked around.

Or maybe not so alone. A shadow at the end of the hallway caught her attention and set her heart to racing. She slipped inside the dressing room and shut the door. Thankfully, two other rodeo clowns were there and in the process of getting ready. Jeanine and Claire.

Was she being paranoid? Tonya didn't chastise herself for it. She had every right to be. Lifting her chin, she moved to an empty table with a mirror over it. She'd made her decision.

She was going to fight back.

"Which routine are you doing today, Tonya?"

"I'm getting shot out of the cannon." She tossed a smile at Claire. The pretty blonde mother of three was new and seemed nervous to work the crowd. She was an amazing bullfighter, though, and Tonya figured she'd soon be winning competitions.

Tonya dressed and applied her makeup while her thoughts spun. Remorse gripped her by the throat. She shouldn't have pushed Seth away so hard. He'd just been trying to help her. She'd apologize as soon as she saw him again.

"I figured that's the act you were doing today," Claire said. "I saw the guys testing the dummy with the cannon."

Tonya nodded. Being shot out of a cannon was a life-and-death act. It wasn't the shooting so much as the landing. She had to land in the net. Which meant the cannon had to be tested to make sure the distance to the net was correctly measured. She felt secure in the act. In fact, it was one of her favorites.

"How do you do that without losing your breakfast?" Claire asked.

Tonya let out a little laugh. "I love the feel of flying through the air. It's a natural rush."

Claire shook her head. "Not me. Thanks." The woman left and Tonya pushed away from the mirror. She was ready. She just prayed if Hank Newman was out there, she saw him before he saw her.

Seth wasn't sure he was ready for the ride and that worried him. He kept fixating on Tonya's curtness and her apparent disregard when he expressed concern for her safety. It bothered him, but he had to push it aside and concentrate on the ride. He grabbed his rope and headed for the bull pen.

He scanned each face he passed, looking for a match to the picture he'd seen of Hank Newman. But he didn't see him.

"Howdy, Seth." Jake stood at the entrance to the bull pen, hands working the rosin onto the rope where he'd grip it during his ride.

"How you doing this morning, Jake?"

"Better than you. That leg bothering you?"

"A bit."

"Going to ride anyway." Seth offered his friend a tight smile. Jake's words hadn't been a question.

Monty poked his head up from the rope he'd been working with. "Mia said Tonya had some excitement last night."

"Yes, a bit."

"She all right?"

"She will be."

Monty glanced at Seth's leg. "Hope you know what you're doing."

Seth sighed. "You and me both. Do you mind—?"

"Attention, folks, may I have your attention." Seth paused as the voice came over the PA system. "The rodeo is canceled for today. I repeat, the rodeo is canceled for today. Please make your way out of the arena. We will let you know when we will be back up and running, but for now, we need you to leave the arena."

Seth frowned. Jake's jaw dropped. Their eyes met. "What? Are they nuts?" Jake asked. "Canceling the rodeo?"

Seth shook his head. "I don't know, but I'm going to find out."

He gathered his bag from the hook where he'd hung it. Then pulled his phone from the bottom and checked it. Clay, his brother, had called three times. Seth hit the button to return the call.

"Seth, finally," Clay said after picking up halfway through the first ring.

Fear sliced through him. "What's wrong? Is everyone okay?"

"Everyone's fine at home. I'm at the arena. I was going to watch you ride—or talk you out of it after I talked to Mom last night—but I got a call from a buddy of mine here in Nashville."

"Yeah?"

"There's been a bomb threat, Seth. You need to get out. *Now.*"

Seth's breath caught. "Seriously?" His thoughts immediately went to Tonya.

"Yeah, the bomb squad is on the way."

"I just heard the announcement. They canceled the rodeo."

"Get out."

"Wait. Where are you?"

"I was heading to the bull pen to find you when you finally called me back."

Seth raised his head and glanced around. Jake had a big question mark on his face. "Hold on a second, Clay." To Jake and Monty, he said, "Keep it quiet, but there's been a bomb threat." Alarm flashed on his friends' faces.

"So *that's* why they pulled the plug on the rodeo," Jake mused.

"Yeah, apparently. We've got to clear out, but I've got to find Tonya first."

"I'll look for her as I head out," Jake offered, already moving.

Monty wasn't far behind him. "I've got to get Mia. If I see Tonya, I'll holler at you."

Seth nodded his thanks. Back on the phone with Clay, he said, "I'm going to climb up on the rail of the fence. See if you can spot me." He grasped the rail and hauled himself up, taking care not to depend on his injured leg to help maintain his balance. Then he looked over the leaving crowd. So far, they were still calm. Disappointed and disgruntled, but not fearful and running, as they would be if they knew the reason for the rodeo's cancellation. And no one was getting hurt because of a human stampede. He just hoped the bomb threat was a hoax.

"I see you," Clay said. "Stay there and we'll get out together."

Seth climbed carefully down from the rail and Clay pushed through the crowd to reach his side. Seth wrapped him in a short man hug, but his brother pushed him away. "Let's go."

"I can't. I've got to find Tonya."

"Who?" Clay asked.

"Tonya Waters. A friend."

Clay frowned. "She'll be leaving, too. No one's going to stay in this arena."

Except possibly the man who was after Tonya and would be watching for her to leave, waiting to grab her under the cover of the crowd. The thought festered inside him and he shook his head. He pulled out his phone and dialed her number.

No answer. He hung up and tried again. Nothing. "I've got to look for her."

"Then I'm coming with you. The cops aren't going to let anyone go in. They're arriving as we speak but trying to be subtle until most of the crowd is gone. If these people panic, it could get ugly." He dug into his pocket and pulled out a black leather wallet-shaped item. "At least I've got a badge. It's gotten me this far. Let's go."

Tonya and several of her coworkers followed the crowd. Confusion and worry churned through her. Why would they cancel the rodeo? It didn't make sense. Obviously something had happened, but what?

She moved quickly through the hall toward the exit. She examined each male face, her eyes landing on one after another. Most talked to one another, asking for information and wondering at the strangeness of the canceled event. Tonya didn't talk. She watched.

She reached in her pocket for her phone, then grimaced when she realized she'd left it on the vanity table. She'd been ready to leave the dressing room and go climb in the barrel of the cannon when the announcement of the cancellation came over the loudspeaker.

Her eyes landed on a familiar figure at the end of the

hall and she came to an abrupt stop. Someone bumped into her from behind but she ignored it as her heart thumped out a faster rhythm.

Hank Newman waited at the exit ahead. In order to get out of the building, she'd have to pass right by him. So far, she didn't think he'd spotted her. Panic assailed her. What should she do?

Tonya turned around and pushed her way against the crowd. "Sorry. Excuse me. Forgot my phone…"

The announcement came over the loudspeaker once more. "Please exit the arena immediately. You may apply for a refund or a ticket exchange online at the rodeo website, but for now, please leave the arena as quickly and safely as possible."

Something was definitely going on and she had a feeling Hank Newman had a hand in it.

SIX

Seth wove his way through the people still pouring out of the arena. "This is impossible," he said to Clay. He had to raise his voice to be heard over the noise.

"Call her again."

"I did. She's not answering."

He dodged another person, an older man in a wheelchair. Law enforcement had descended and was helping guide the people and make sure order reigned. Most people probably assumed the cops were there to keep everything under control. But those who noticed would question the bomb-squad van that had pulled up at the front.

"Excuse me, gentlemen, you're going the wrong way."

Seth stopped at the officer's upraised hand. Clay pulled his badge and held it up. "He's with me."

The policeman frowned but nodded and let them through. Clay's badge might not have read Nashville, but it did have Tennessee on it and people parted to make way for them. Seth kept moving toward the building where he'd left Tonya not too long ago. Thankfully, the crowd had thinned considerably.

"Seth!"

He spun toward the familiar voice. "Tonya?"

She'd come from the opposite end of the building. Not the exit he'd expected to see her appear from. She ran toward him dressed in full bullfighting gear. "He's here," she panted.

"Who? Hank?"

She nodded, her fear palpable. He turned to his brother. "Clay, this is Tonya." Clay shook her hand and Seth slipped an arm around her shoulders. "It's okay. Let's go. We'll talk more once we're away from here."

He started to lead her away, not wanting to tell her about the bomb scare yet.

They hurried toward the nearest exit.

"Tonya Waters?" Clay stopped and pulled her to a halt. Her attention swung from Seth to the officer who'd stepped up to them. He checked his phone, then took another close look at Tonya.

"Yes, I'm Tonya."

"Can you come with me, please?"

She blinked. "Why?"

"We'd like to ask you a few questions."

Clay stepped forward and flashed his badge once more. "What's this about?"

The officer nodded and motioned to them. "I'm not exactly sure. I just got a notification to look for this woman." He turned the phone around. Two pictures of Tonya side by side were on the screen. One had her driver's-license picture; the other had her dressed in her bullfighting attire—which was the only reason the officer had recognized her. The bright shirt, red wig and makeup stood out. "Just follow me," he said.

Seth could feel the tension emanating from Tonya. She lifted her chin and took off after the officer. Her gaze swung from left to right, and Seth knew she was looking for Hank.

The officer led them out of the arena and to a police cruiser. "Would you get in, please?"

Tonya backpedaled. "Not until I get an explanation," she said.

"That's right, Officer." Clay stepped forward. "You're going to have to be a little more forthcoming."

The cop sighed. "Just a minute." He moved about ten feet away and spoke into his radio.

"What's going on?" Tonya whispered.

Clay shook his head. "I don't know. But I'll say it probably has something to do with the bomb threat."

Tonya sucked in air. "Bomb threat? What bomb threat?"

"The reason the arena was evacuated," Seth whispered back. A tremor ran through her and he drew her closer.

"And the reason that officer walked us all the way out here away from the area," Clay added.

The officer returned. "All right, some of the higher-ups want to ask you some questions about the bomb found in your cannon."

The sky tilted and Tonya thought she might be in serious danger of passing out. Only Seth's hold on her upper arm kept her from crashing into the dirt. She stared at the police officer, mouth agape. "What?"

He hitched his belt a little higher and stroked his chin. "One of the guys who's on your setup team found it. Said he was going to check the spring one more time. He dropped the dummy into the barrel but it wouldn't go all the way down. He pulled the dummy out and found the device. Scared him to death. He was on his knees thanking the Lord it didn't go off."

Tonya couldn't seem to stop shaking. They'd found a bomb. In *her* cannon. Someone could have been killed. "Maybe it's a prank. Just a stupid joke."

"The bomb squad is there now and will determine

that. We've got bomb dogs going all through the facility. But the main question we want to ask is, who would do this? Do you have any idea who would put a bomb in your cannon?"

"Hank Newman," she whispered. "He would." She covered her mouth with her fingers. "This has to stop. I have to stop him. But how?"

"By letting the authorities find him," Seth said in a firm tone.

"I'll take a leave of absence immediately." As much as she hated to do it, Tonya knew it was the right thing to do. Innocent people could have been hurt. Maybe even killed. She shook her head. "I'll get in my motor home and disappear."

"No, he'll just find you," Seth said. "You've been running for a while now, haven't you?"

"Ever since he got out of prison."

"Then maybe it's time for a new game plan. What do you think about finding a way to put him away for good instead of always having to look over your shoulder?"

Tonya rubbed her eyes. "That would be ideal, of course, but I don't know how to do that. Even when he violates a restraining order, he manages to turn it around. And the cops believe him. You can't touch him."

"Why?"

"Because he comes from a family of law enforcement."

Clay lifted a brow. "He went to prison before."

"Because I had irrefutable proof. He won't make that mistake again. He acted on impulse when he tried to strangle me. He was angry and lost his cool. This time he'll be careful, very careful."

The officer stepped forward. "Where were you during the testing of the cannon?" he asked.

"What do you mean?"

"Someone always does a test run on the cannon before you get into it, right?"

"Yes."

"Where were you while this was going on?"

"Getting ready." She gestured to herself. "Putting this outfit on. Painting my face. Why?"

"They'll want to rule you out as a suspect," Clay said quietly.

"Oh." Tonya grabbed the wig and pulled it off. Her blond ponytail tumbled down her back. "I didn't put that bomb in there. From the moment I stepped in the arena, I've been around people who can vouch for my whereabouts."

"Could you give me some names?"

"Of course." She rattled them off and the officer's pen scratched across the paper. His radio crackled and he listened. Tonya couldn't make out the words. When it stopped, he nodded and shut his notebook. "No one has come across Mr. Newman yet. We'll keep him on the radar, though."

"He's here." She clasped her arms and hugged herself while she kept glancing around. Even though they were a good distance away, she could see the area still teemed with law enforcement, but it looked as though most of the rodeo goers had left.

"You don't think he would have left with the crowd?"

Tonya shuddered. "I don't know. I just know I want to get out of here before he shows back up."

Seth rubbed his chin and gave her a thoughtful look. "The next rodeo I'm competing in isn't for another two weeks," he said. She knew he rode in only the ones that offered the biggest cash payouts.

"What's your point?"

"Come home with me."

She stilled, frowned. "What?"

"We've got two weeks." He looked at Clay. "Can you find this guy if she hides out at Mom and Dad's house?"

Clay stared back for a moment. Something seemed to pass between the two men. Then he nodded. "Obviously I can't promise anything, but we can do our best." He scrubbed a hand over his face. "I have a lot of resources I can put to good use. Shouldn't be that much trouble to get him."

Tonya started to protest, then scanned the arena in the distance. Someone had put a bomb in her cannon. If one of the workers hadn't exercised some extra caution, she'd be dead—possibly along with some innocent bystanders. She turned back to Seth. "Fine. If it's what I need to do to make sure no one gets hurt." She bit her lip, her gaze bouncing between the three men. "What about your parents? What if this person manages to find me? Your family could be in danger."

"It wouldn't be the first time," Clay muttered.

Tonya lifted a brow and Seth flexed his jaw. "I'll explain that comment later. For now, Hank wouldn't have any reason to know you'd go to Wrangler's Corner. You should be perfectly safe there while we figure out what to do about your stalker."

Ice slid up her spine. Indecision gnawed at her. "I don't think that's possible." She sighed. "Seth, I have four older brothers. I won't even go to one of them, because of the threats Hank made against them. If I haven't asked them for help, how can I risk your family?"

"Think about it. It makes sense that you would go to a family member for sanctuary. Hank knows your family. He might even watch them to see if that's where you go after he realizes his plan here has failed." He looked around. "Which he already knows at this point. But when he doesn't find you with your family, he'll realize you went somewhere else. Only by then you'll be at the ranch and he'll have no way to track you."

It sounded good. It even sounded reasonable. She didn't really want to chance it, but what else could she do? "All right. We'll try it, but at the first sign of danger, I'm out of there."

"Don't worry. It'll be all right. We'll find Hank, get him put back behind bars, and all will be well."

Somehow those words didn't hold as much comfort as Seth probably intended. She had no doubt he fully believed what he'd just said, but there was only one problem.

She knew Hank and he didn't.

SEVEN

Seth checked his rearview mirror one more time. Tonya was right behind him as he turned onto the back road that would lead him to his family's ranch in Wrangler's Corner, Tennessee. He loved the rodeo, but he had to admit, he loved coming home just as much. He'd called ahead to make sure it was all right with his mother. She'd been slightly insulted he'd felt the need to ask. "Of course you can bring your friend here. It's not like we haven't faced down a little danger before and lived to tell about it."

A little over eight months ago, his older brother Steven had been murdered. Clay had come home to find the killer and grieve with the rest of the family. He'd wound up taking a deputy position on the small Wrangler's Corner police force. When the sheriff and family friend had been found guilty of being behind the murder, Clay had been promoted to sheriff. And now Seth was bringing the possibility of danger back into his family's lives.

And yet he really did believe they'd be all right. After all, how would Hank know where to look for Tonya? The only connection Seth and Tonya shared was the rodeo. There was no way he would think to search for Tonya in Wrangler's Corner.

Would he?

Seth couldn't deny the sliver of unease that continued to nag at him, but Tonya needed help and he was determined to give it to her. He just wasn't ready to delve into all the reasons why.

He pulled into the drive of the ranch and angled his fifth wheel around to the spot reserved for his visits. The main house sat to his left, the barn out beyond that. There were six cottages down by one of the large ponds that his family rented out during peak season. He let his eyes move past them. Rolling green pastures as far as the eye could see immediately sent peace flooding through him. He hoped the place had the same effect on Tonya. Putting the truck in Park, he drew in a steadying breath, preparing himself for the pain of moving his leg. He supposed he should be thankful it was his left one and not the one he needed in order to be able to drive.

Taking his time, he climbed out, clenching his jaw against the jabbing reminder that it was probably a good thing he didn't have to ride today. He motioned for Tonya to park beside him.

She did and just sat there. He limped over to her and could see her fingers wrapped around the steering wheel, her knuckles white, her face pinched. Second thoughts, he figured.

He tapped the window and she jumped, then opened the door. "You okay?" he asked.

"I'm fine. Just still torn as to whether this is the right decision or not. Are you sure Hank couldn't have followed?"

"No way. Clay drove behind us, watching for any tails. At the last turn, he called and said we were in the clear. He's going into the office to see if there's anything he can find out."

Tonya inhaled deeply and let it out slowly, then gave him a jerky nod. "All right, then."

He took her hand and squeezed her fingers. Then let go. "Come on. I'll introduce you." He started for the front door.

"Seth?"

He turned to see his father exit the barn, a welcoming smile on his face. "Dad. Hey there." He took a step and gritted his teeth to keep the grimace off his face.

His father reached him and embraced him. "Good to see you." He glanced at Seth's leg. "How's it feel?"

"Lousy." The word slipped out before he could edit it. "I'm all right, though." Seth nodded to Tonya before his dad could comment. "I'd like you to meet a friend of mine. Tonya Waters. Tonya, this is my dad, Ross Starke."

His father and Tonya shook hands. "Nice to meet you, sir."

"Likewise. I've seen you bull-fight some of Seth's rides. It's always a relief to see you in the arena with him."

Pink crept into her cheeks. "Thank you—I appreciate that."

"Seth? You're home!" This time it was his mother's voice calling to him. She rushed from the front porch across the stretch of dirt and stopped in front of him. He knew she wanted to grab him in one of her bear hugs but didn't want to risk hurting him.

He smiled and leaned over to plant a kiss on her head. "Hi, Mom." She frowned and looked at his leg. He could see the question forming on her lips. "It's fine."

"Hmm. I doubt that." But she let him get away with it, turning her attention to Tonya. He made the introductions and his mother linked her arm through Tonya's.

"Come on inside and we'll have a glass of tea and get to know one another. The boys can take care of the bags."

"Oh, Seth said you had hookups, so I'm just going to stay in my motor home."

The woman clucked and shook her head as she led the way into the kitchen. "You're just like Seth. He likes his own space, too." She hustled toward the cabinet and started pulling down glasses. "Iced tea?"

"That would be wonderful, thank you," Tonya said. It wasn't so much a matter of liking her own space; it was worry about putting Seth's family out and being an inconvenience. Although no one had even hinted at that.

"We still need to get that bathroom light fixed for you," Seth said. He looked at his mother. "I had someone lined up to come fix it at the arena, but we left before it could be done."

She waved a hand in dismissal. "I'm sure Larry will be happy to take care of it."

"That's who I was thinking of." He settled himself at the table and Tonya did the same. She leaned back in the chair and let herself start to relax. Maybe this was the right decision after all.

The door opened and Seth's father stepped into the kitchen. He went to the sink and washed his hands and face. "It's hot out there."

"Too hot for you to be working so hard," Seth's mother said. She handed him a glass of tea and he downed it in one gulp. While she refilled it and put together a lunch of ham sandwiches, chips and fresh fruit, he studied Tonya. Then let his gaze slide to his son, then back to her. Tonya thought she saw a glimmer of respect enter the man's eyes. "Bullfighting's a pretty dangerous job. How'd you get into it?"

In a rare moment, Tonya let her mind drift back to

her childhood. "I have four older brothers. We grew up in Montana on a ranch. We had an ornery old bull and my brothers insisted on riding it when my parents were otherwise occupied."

"Uh-oh."

"Yes, there were a lot of 'uh-ohs.'" Tonya smiled, the memories of her family warming her. She usually refused to allow herself to think about them as it just made her feel sad and long to go home. But sharing with Seth's parents felt good. "They're great guys, but they're all older than I am, so I never got to be the bull rider, just the clown."

Seth frowned. "Weren't they concerned you'd get hurt?"

She shrugged and bit into the sandwich Seth's mother had placed in front of her. After she swallowed, she said, "We didn't really think about it, to be honest. I just had a good time running from the bull and flipping over the fence when I had to get out of the way. I got nicked by his horns a couple of times but, unbelievably enough, nothing too serious happened."

She chuckled. "When I was fourteen, my mother found out what I was doing and she was livid. She'd come home from work early just in time to see my brother Grant get tossed from the back of the bull and me rush out and distract it while my other brothers got Grant out of the way. When she could speak again, she grounded the boys for about six months and enrolled me in gymnastics five days a week so I wouldn't have time to play rodeo clown."

"But you came back to it."

She nodded. "I love it. It's a great profession. Only I did it the right way this time. I got the training I needed to be as safe as possible. The people are interesting and I can honestly say I'm never bored."

"She's good at it, too," Seth told his parents. "Saved

my hide yesterday." His mother flinched and his father frowned. Tonya bit her lip and wondered why he'd blurted that out.

His mother walked over and gave Tonya a hug. "Then we're forever in your debt. Anything you need, you just ask for."

Tonya returned the hug, missing her mom more than ever right now. "Thank you, Mrs. Starke. I'm sure I'll be just fine."

The woman wiped her eyes. "It's Julianna. Finish your lunch."

"And I'm Ross." Tonya noted his voice had gone a little deeper. As though his throat had tightened with emotion and he had to force the words out. "Now, why don't you tell us a little about this trouble you're in?"

Seth cleared his throat. "Tonya has a stalker, Dad. He tried to kill her at the rodeo last night and this morning. I told her she could come here while the police try to track him down."

His father blanched and concern knit his brows together. "Oh, my dear. Of course."

"But at the first sign of danger, I'm gone… I promise. I would never want to do anything to bring harm to your family."

"You don't worry about that. We'll be just fine," Ross said. He reached over to clasp her hand.

Seth nodded. "Clay's at the office working on it even as we speak."

"Well, then." Ross pulled his gloves from his back pocket and stood. "I'm going to get back out to the barn and finish mucking the stalls."

"Where's Jordan?" Seth asked. Jordan Zellis, the young teen Steven had taken under his wing before his death. Now Jordan and his younger brother and sister lived with Clay and his wife, Sabrina. The adoption was in progress and looked as if it was going to happen without any drama. Which would be a relief for everyone.

"He's at the lake with a few of his friends from the youth group." His dad winked. "Can't be all work and no play around here, you know."

Seth nodded and stood. "All right, I'm going to give Larry a call and see if he can get out here today." He looked at Tonya. "Let's go get the information off your motor home so I know what to tell him to bring."

Seth limped his way to the door and Tonya followed him. Outside, the afternoon heat hit her and she blinked at the bright sunlight. They walked over to the motor home. She pulled her phone from her pocket and stared at it. "What's put that frown on your face?" he asked. "Besides the obvious, I mean." He had one foot on the step.

She grimaced. "I don't watch a lot of television but even I know I can be tracked through my phone. Hank knows the name I've been using for the past four years now. He can trace my phone, my credit cards. Everything."

Seth blinked. "Tonya Waters isn't your real name?"

She shook her head. "I'm Tonya Rene Lewis."

"Oh. So how did you get all of those government-issued cards in the name you're using now?"

She gave him a tight smile. "My brother Grant has a friend who's a US marshal. When Grant told her what was going on, she was more than willing to help me."

"Nice."

"I thought so." She returned the phone to her pocket without dialing. "But now I'm phoneless and penniless. He'll be watching my bank accounts, too."

"How can he do that?"

"He has friends in high places. And law enforcement,

too. He even managed to track me down after I used a friend's cell phone to call home."

Seth cocked his head. "He couldn't have traced the friend's number, so that means..."

"Exactly. Somehow he's watching my parents' number and tracing the calls that come in."

"This guy is a piece of work." He reached for her hand. "Okay, here's what we're going to do. I'll loan you whatever you need. You can pay me back when this is all over if you insist."

He thought he saw a sheen of tears glaze over her eyes as she nodded. "Which I will. But thanks. I guess I'm going to have to take you up on that, aren't I?"

"Yes, you are." He stepped back down. "It's hard for you to ask for help, isn't it?"

She huffed out a breath. "It is."

"Why?"

Her right shoulder lifted. "I guess because of how I grew up. Four older brothers. Four very *protective* older brothers. Sometimes I felt smothered. I've had to fight and scrap for every ounce of independence I got. Of course, the whole thing with Hank fueled that fire."

"Of course it would. But it doesn't sound like they were too protective if they were letting you be the bull-fighter in the family."

She gave him a wry smile. "I know. It's weird. They didn't want a boy within five feet of me. If I went out with my friends, I had to check in at the appointed time or they'd be in town looking for me. But they cheered me on when I got in the arena with a wild animal that could squash me like a bug."

"Could they have stopped you from doing it?"

"Probably not. At least not until my parents found out. Like I mentioned, they were horrified. But my brothers thought it was awesome. They even snuck me to a bull-fighters' competition the minute I turned eighteen." She gave him a half smile. "I won and have been doing it ever since."

"You have a definite knack for it." He climbed into the motor home. She joined him and found a packet of information on the vehicle. Soon he had the numbers he needed and dialed Larry. "Larry owned the RV Stop and Shop about fifteen minutes outside Wrangler's Corner."

The man answered on the third ring. "Now, I have to say I'm surprised to see your number pop up on my screen," he said.

Seth smiled. "Come on. It hasn't been that long."

Larry grunted. "Long enough. What you need?"

Without going into a lot of detail, Seth told him the reason for the call. He sent him the pictures he'd taken, as well. "You think you could get out here sometime today and fix it?"

"If I have the parts. Let me just take a look at the picture and get the info from your text. Hold on." In less than a minute Seth heard the keys of a keyboard clicking. "Well, looks like you're a winner today. I've got everything in stock. It'll take me some time to get it together and get out there, though. I've got another job ahead of you. I can come see you first thing in the morning."

"Tomorrow's Saturday. You don't take the weekend off?"

"Now, Seth, you know I never turn down the opportunity to make some money. Now, if y'all will be up bright and early, I'll be there."

"That works. We'll be up."

"All righty, then. See you around eight."

"See you then." Seth hung up and turned to find Tonya staring at a picture she held in her hands. "What's that?"

She looked up. "A picture of my family. I miss them."

A simple statement that said a lot. "I'm sure you do. When's the last time you saw them?"

"Shortly after Hank got out of prison. I was at the ranch and he came by looking for me. My brother Patrick told him to get lost."

"And he did?"

"Not without leaving a parting shot."

"Which was?"

"A cliché. He had on a jacket. He pushed it back and I could see the gun in his waistband." Her voice quivered as she forced the words out.

Seth moved to her side and took her hand. "And?"

"Then he proceeded to tell Patrick that he couldn't stop him, that they couldn't protect me forever and he'd have me one way or another. Or if he couldn't have me, nobody else would either. Including my family."

EIGHT

It might have been a cliché, but she'd taken Hank at his word and acted accordingly. Seth slipped his arms around and just held her. She relished the closeness, his musky scent and strong arms. If only she could hold on to this moment for the rest of her life. But she couldn't. She moved away and felt a pang at the separation. He dropped his arms but didn't back away. "What happened after that?" he asked.

"The next day Hank showed up at my office and I left before he saw me. I convinced my family I needed to leave town, that they would be in danger if I stayed."

"You really think they would have been?"

"Definitely. They tried to talk me out of it, of course, but I'd made up my mind." She shook her head. "I knew what I had to do. When they realized I was going with or without their blessing, Grant made me promise to stick around long enough to get the new identity and paperwork."

"Good for him."

"That took a day and a half. I left the night I had it, slipping away when everyone was sleeping. I didn't want one of them trying to play hero and follow me." She blew out a breath. "Plus, I wanted them clueless because I knew Hank would be back. They'd have nothing to tell him because they wouldn't know anything."

"Do they know where you are now?"

She sighed. "I suspect Grant does. Every Christmas I find a box of my favorite gourmet chocolates on the steps to my motor home."

"So he's keeping tabs on you."

She pulled her phone out and waved it at him. "Probably. He knows the alias I'm using. I doubt it was very hard for him to find me. As soon as I turned this on, Grant was having it tracked."

"You took comfort in that." His voice was soft.

"I did." And it didn't make her feel smothered. Which she appreciated. Tonya moved to the couch and sat down. She'd left the air conditioner on and the interior was nice and cool. The black tarp they'd tacked over the bathroom ceiling was doing its job. She'd be fine living in her motor home until Larry was able to get out here and fix the light. "So tell me about your family. I've met Clay."

Seth nodded. "He's two years older than I am. He married Sabrina Mayfield last month." He smiled. "They're in the process of adopting three foster children."

"Wow. That's a lot to take on."

"They're up to it. My eldest brother, Steven, was killed a little over eight months ago."

She blanched. "I'm so sorry."

"I am, too. The sheriff, one of my dad's best friends, was behind it. It was all related to drugs." He shook his head and grief flashed across his face. "Such a waste."

"That's awful."

"And then there's Aaron. He graduated just before Clay and Sabrina's wedding. He's now an official veterinarian and is working in town with Dr. Thatcher. Doc

T wants to retire in a couple of years and has his eye on Aaron to take over the practice."

"And you have a sister."

A frown flickered across his face. "Yes. Then there's Amber, my younger sister."

"Why the frown?"

"We just can't figure her out."

Tonya lifted a brow. "What does she do?"

"She's a writer for a travel magazine. She's very successful, too, if you go by all the articles she's putting out, but—" he shrugged "—the last time I spoke to her was at Christmastime. She missed Clay's wedding and Aaron's graduation."

"Oh. What a shame."

"Yeah. All she would say was that she had last-minute assignments she couldn't get out of." He took a deep breath. "I don't know about you, but I'm exhausted. I'm going to go put my leg up and—as much as it goes against my nature—take my doctor's advice and go easy on it today."

Tonya nodded. A nap sounded lovely. "I'll be right here."

"And I'll let you know if Clay comes up with anything regarding Hank."

She grimaced. "Thanks."

He limped to the door, hesitated and came back to stand in front of her. "It's going to be all right." He traced a finger down her cheek and this time her shivers had nothing to do with the fact that she had a stalker after her.

"I appreciate that. And everything else you're doing."

He leaned over and kissed her forehead. When he pulled back, she caught her breath. "You're very welcome."

Then he turned and made his way out, shutting the door behind him. He was in pain. The lack of color in his face and the fact that he was even talking about taking it easy said more than his words did.

Tonya rubbed her eyes and contemplated the fact that Seth was beginning to mean more to her than just a friend. She knew the feeling was mutual. The question was, would anything come from it? Unfortunately, she just didn't know. She pulled her phone from her pocket once again. She needed to give Grant a heads-up that Hank had found her, but now that she felt relatively safe, she didn't want to take a chance that her ex could trace her cell phone. He certainly had the resources.

After puttering and cleaning and thinking, she finally moved to the back of the motor home, lay on the bed and closed her eyes even while her mind spun. How *had* Hank found her after all this time? What had given her away? She hadn't been working the rodeo circuit when they'd met. Her senior year, she'd had to focus on her studies, and fortunately, between her scholarships and her savings, she hadn't had to work that last year. What was more, she knew she hadn't even mentioned working as a bullfighter to Hank. She avoided the topic as it seemed intimidating to most guys. But even though she hadn't shared her passion with Hank, some of her friends knew. One of them could have said something to him if he'd gone around seeking them out.

She sighed, felt herself relax almost against her will. She desperately needed sleep. But her mind tried to fight the weariness of her body. She had to stay alert, be watching and waiting, because no matter what Seth thought, Tonya knew Hank would be coming sooner or later.

Seth sat at his mother's kitchen table, leg propped up on the chair beside him. He pressed the phone to his ear. "Hi, Lance." Lance Goode was a deputy with the Wrangler's Corner sheriff's department. He'd become a good friend of the family's ever since his ex-wife, Krissy, had been arrested for kidnapping and being complicit with the sheriff in Steven's murder.

"Clay said you were back."

"Yeah."

"He also said you had a houseguest who was in a bit of trouble."

"Her name is Tonya Waters. Did you or Clay find anything?"

"Maybe. Clay went to deal with a fight that broke out at the feed store but said you needed this info ASAP."

"That's right," Seth said. "So what have you got?"

"Well, apparently Hank Newman was squeaky-clean as a teenager but seemed to develop a mean streak when he hit college. Dated one girl and put her in the hospital. She dropped the charges and Newman walked. His next victim has the same story."

"Tonya said his family was in law enforcement."

"Yes. Quite a few members in different branches," Lance confirmed.

"If they don't believe him capable of the things he's been accused of, they would pull strings and call in favors to help him stay out of jail."

"Or even if they *do* believe him guilty, they might still be tempted to use their position to protect him. Even cover for him." Lance cleared his throat. "He's family, after all. His uncle is a chief of police and golfing buddies with congressmen and the attorney general of Montana."

"Those are some mighty-powerful friends." Seth paused. "Tonya grew up there."

"So did Hank Newman."

Seth sighed. Weariness settled like a mantle over his

shoulders. "All right. Thanks. No word on Newman's whereabouts?"

"According to my reports, Tonya said she saw him at the rodeo, but his office said he was away at a conference."

"What kind of conference?"

"The guy is an accountant," Lance replied. "He works for his brother's firm in Billings and he's supposed to be attending some conference in Orlando."

"Did he show up?"

"I called and they've got him as having checked in. He picked up his badge and it looks like he's there."

"Looks like." Doubt crept in. Had Tonya really seen Hank Newman or had she just thought she had? "Text me a picture of the guy, will you? I ran into someone at the rodeo who was in a restricted area. Tonya was hiding from him. Let me see if it's the same guy."

"Okay. And I'll keep working on my end."

"Thanks, Lance." Seth ended the call and looked up to find his mother watching him. "Hi."

"I didn't mean to eavesdrop."

"Of course not."

"Okay, so maybe a little." Her lips quirked in a half smile.

Seth's phone beeped. He tapped the screen and a male in his mid- to late twenties faced him. Dark brown hair, brown eyes, smooth complexion with slight five o'clock shadow. He would say the man was good-looking and could see that women might be attracted to him. But was he the person he'd run into in the storage room?

Possibly, but the guy in the storage room had shaggy hair, a mustache and a goatee. Still…

"Is it him?"

He looked up from his phone. "I can't tell. Could be."

"That poor girl. We have to keep her safe."

Yes. Yes, they did.

* * *

Tonya woke Saturday morning disoriented and with a sinus headache that wouldn't quit. After downing three ibuprofen and two cups of coffee, she decided she might live to fight back against Hank Newman.

A microwaved biscuit and two pieces of questionable ham from her fridge topped off her breakfast. She needed to get to a grocery store. Sighing, she went back to the window and peered out. Rolling land, cattle grazing, horses nibbling the grass. It was a beautiful piece of land and reminded her of home. A home she couldn't go to because of Hank. Just the thought of him made her fingers shake with a suppressed rage. He had no right to do this to her. One more check to make sure that nothing was out of place, no one was watching her and waiting for her to step out of the motor home so he could pounce, convinced her she was truly safe for the moment.

She turned on her laptop, set up her Wi-Fi and sent an email to her eldest brother, Grant.

Hank Newman showed up at the rodeo in Nashville, Tennessee. I'm all right but am on the run again. I'm safe right now with friends who have some law-enforcement resources and are helping me. Will be in touch as often as I can. Give Mom and Dad my love.

She hit Send and sent up a prayer for safety. Not just for herself but for her family and Seth's. Although one thing was certain: as long as Hank was chasing her, he wasn't hurting someone in her family.

The knock on her door made her jump. With a pounding heart, she got up and peered out the window. Seth stood there with another man dressed in denim overalls and a Yankees baseball cap. She opened the door. "Good morning."

"Morning," Seth said. "Tonya, this is Larry. He's here to fix your bathroom light."

"Come on in." She let him find his own way and drank in the sight of Seth settling himself on her couch. She could get used to having him around. Not just because he was a good-looking man with his broad shoulders, blue eyes and heart-stopping smile—although that certainly didn't hurt—but because when he was in her space she felt protected, cared for. Weird how her brothers' protection used to drive her crazy, but she didn't seem to mind Seth's protective instincts. "How's the leg?"

"Painful, but not as bad as yesterday. My doc called in a physical therapy prescription to the woman I was seeing when I recovered from my first fall. I have an appointment Monday after lunch."

"Good. I think that's probably a wise thing to do."

He grunted. "I suppose."

She ran a hand through her hair. "I don't suppose you'd let me borrow your truck, would you?"

He frowned. "Well, of course I would, but where do you need to go?"

"I need some supplies, like food and shampoo, and wanted to run into town."

"I don't mind taking you."

She gave a slow nod. "Okay, that would be great. When can you be ready to go?"

"Fifteen minutes?"

"Let me check on Larry's progress and I'll let you know."

"Sounds like a plan." He stood up and headed for the door, his limp there, but the pain *did* seem to be better. Tonya stood for a moment and just watched him. And felt her heart slip a little further out of her control. "Remember Daniel," she whispered.

"What was that?" Seth asked.

She blinked. "Nothing. I'll be right back."

She found Larry climbing down from the roof. "How's it going?"

"I've got everything in place here. I just need to get another part from my truck to finish it up. It'll just take me about thirty minutes more and I'll be out of your hair."

"Oh, that was fast."

He shrugged. "Nothing to it, really."

"All right. Thanks. How much do I owe you?"

"Not a penny. Seth took care of it."

Tonya caught her jaw before it dropped. "Oh right." She'd just put it on the tab. Anger at Hank stirred anew and she couldn't wait to see the man behind bars, where he belonged.

NINE

Twenty minutes later, Tonya found herself sitting next to Seth once again. The ride down the mountain was blissfully uneventful even though she couldn't help watching the mirrors. She noticed Seth doing the same. Her actions were habit; his were newly formed, thanks to her. She grimaced.

He pulled into the parking lot and she read the sign above the front door. "'WC Groceries.' WC? Wrangler's Corner?"

"Wilson Carlisle. He's part of one of the founding families of this town. His great-grandfather ran a general store back in the eighteen hundreds. Wilson and I went to high school together. He's a good guy." He put the truck in Park. "Do you mind if I run next door and fill up while you get what you need?"

"That's fine."

"I'll be right here when you come back out."

She nodded and slipped out of the vehicle. Seth drove off and she stopped to read the flyer on the glass door about the rodeo.

Tonya entered the store with a little jingle. She smiled when she spotted the bell tied to the handle on the inside. How old-fashioned. And refreshing. The whole town was quaint and charming and she could feel it growing on her already. Almost like an instant connection of feeling as if she belonged. And for two whole seconds she forgot Hank Newman and the threat he presented.

Her smile slipped into a frown as the memories rushed back and she grabbed a cart from the rack. "Just get your groceries," she muttered. Then looked around to make sure no one had witnessed her moment of craziness.

A young mother with a toddler on her hip and a baby carrier propped in the cart stood looking at the baby formula on the shelf in front of her.

Tonya moved on to the toiletries aisle and grabbed toothpaste, deodorant and some shampoo. Next she hit the meat department and stocked up on the deli ham and turkey. She had a bread maker in the motor home—

The hairs on her neck spiked and she jerked, looked behind her. No one except a teenager pulling a bag of chicken from the freezer. The teen moved down the aisle while Tonya stayed frozen to her spot. Her eyes scanned as far as she could see. An L-shaped scan from her back corner of the store. She could see up one aisle and down another. There was nothing that should set off her internal alarm. She drew in a deep breath and turned back to the meat. Then stopped.

Ignoring the feeling wasn't an option. She'd learned to pay attention to that survival instinct. But was it Hank or something else?

What else—*who else*—could it be? She moved for a better view of the ends of each aisle. Several people shopped. And then he caught her attention.

A man wearing a baseball cap low on his forehead and dressed in khaki pants and a golf shirt exited one of the far aisles, then turned into the one immediately next to it. Tonya threw the ham in her buggy and pushed the cart toward the man she'd noticed. She ignored the strange looks from other customers and turned into the aisle.

He wasn't there.

She walked to the end, past the canned vegetables, and turned the corner near the registers. Her heart thumped; her breathing quickened. Where had he gone? She moved to the next aisle, then the next. She covered the grocery store without seeing him again. She blinked and felt the tears pool beneath her lashes. Was she losing it?

The doors swished open and Seth stepped inside, his eyes immediately homing in on her like a heat-seeking missile. His brow furrowed and he strode to her. "What's wrong?"

"I think Hank was here."

Seth looked around, then back at her. "Are you sure?"

"Yes." She ran a hand through her hair. "No. I mean, I just caught a glimpse. He was pushing a buggy and turned up the aisle. I went after him to get another look and he disappeared."

"What? You went after him? What were you thinking?"

"That I'm tired of being a victim." Her voice rose and she flinched when two nearby shoppers turned to stare. "Sorry," she said quietly. "I'm just tired of all of this. Frustrated."

"I understand." He settled a hand on her shoulder. "Okay. I'm not saying you didn't see him, but it could have been someone who looked a little like him."

She turned and looked around, then met his intense blue gaze again. "It could have."

"But you don't believe that."

This time she blinked and looked away from him. "I'm sorry, Seth… I don't know what to believe, to be honest.

I didn't imagine the man, but maybe you're right. Maybe he just looked enough like Hank to freak me out since I keep expecting to see him every time I turn around."

"I believe you saw him, but he couldn't just disappear." He gently clasped her wrists, pulling her toward him. "Come on."

"Where?"

"I'm going to check the bathroom." She left the buggy and followed him to the restrooms. He pushed open the door and slipped inside. Two stalls, a sink and a hand dryer were the only occupants. When he exited, Tonya looked ready to bolt. He held up a hand. "It's empty."

Tonya blew out a breath and her shoulders wilted. "I'm glad and mad all at the same time." She wiped her eyes and shook her head. "I'm sorry. I'm being crazy. Let me just get this stuff and we can head back to your place. You're right. There's no way Hank could know where I am."

Seth went through the line with her. "Do you need some cash?"

She held up her debit card. "I suppose I shouldn't use this, should I?"

"No. Not until we know for sure if it was Hank you saw or not." He pulled his card from his wallet and swiped it through the machine. He glanced at her, saw the color in her cheeks and knew she was embarrassed. But he wasn't. He had to admit he liked buying her groceries and he liked watching out for her. He just hated that there was someone out there who truly wanted to harm her.

Tonya took the receipt from the cashier and Seth grabbed the one bag. He cast another look around the store but didn't see anyone resembling the man Tonya had described. Then a thought hit him. "Hey, come with me, will you?"

She blinked. "Okay. What is it?"

"I just want to look at something." He took the bag to the customer-service counter and left it with the permission of the woman stocking the newspapers. He grabbed Tonya's hand and pulled her to the back of the store. He walked one way, then another and thought he might know how the man had disappeared so easily. "Show me the aisle where you saw the guy go."

"Okay." Tonya pointed. "He came out of that one and then went up this way." She demonstrated.

Once Seth had the route down, he told her, "Go stand where you were when you first saw this guy. I'm going to move and I want you to follow me just like you did him, all right?"

Tonya nodded and moved to the meat section in the refrigerated area. He waited for her to stop and turn to catch his eye. Then he pulled back, took a deep breath and walked around the corner of the aisle past the display. He saw Tonya start to move toward him and kept going all the way to the end. He cut left and back down the next aisle.

Tonya went after him at a fast clip, hurrying to catch him. But just like when she followed the other man, when she turned into the aisle, Seth was gone. Even with a bum leg, he'd managed to disappear. She checked one aisle, then the next and the next, and still no sign of Seth. She threw her hands up and waited. Within a minute he came strolling up to her from the back of the store. "Where were you?"

"In the employees-only part of the store. I simply walked up the aisle, turned and walked—" he looked at his leg "—okay, *limped* down the next aisle and pushed through the double doors that lead to the back."

Tonya gaped, then let a humorless laugh escape her. "I didn't even think of that."

"I didn't either until I saw the guy push a cart of salads up to the deli section. While I was back there, I looked. There's a back door that leads out into the alley. He could have slipped right out."

"So he could have been here," she breathed.

"If that's what happened. If it was Hank. It could have been a worker putting something on the shelves. It's all just speculation at this point."

"You sound like a cop."

He gave her a tight smile. "That's what I get for having a brother in law enforcement."

"Well, the guy pushing that buggy wasn't putting stuff on the shelves, but...okay. So what now?"

Seth folded his arms across his chest and locked eyes with her. "Now we let Clay know about this and continue to use caution. Tonight we feast on my mother's pot roast and tomorrow we go to church."

"You go to church?"

He laughed. "When I'm home. And sometimes when I'm on the road. The rodeo life doesn't always lend itself to consistent attendance, but I do what I can."

Tonya's face went red. "I know that. I wasn't being judgmental."

"Didn't think you were. So? You want to go?"

She looked around. "I'd love to, but what if that was Hank?"

"Then I'd say being around people is probably the safest place for you."

"The safest place for me, but what about everyone else?"

Seth thought about that. It was a valid question and spoke to her character that she was still extremely concerned about those around her. "I'd say that at the rodeo, Hank knew exactly where you were going to be and had time to think up a plan and try to carry it out. However, us going to church tomorrow is completely unplanned. He doesn't know you're here, and even if that was him earlier—which I'm having my doubts about—he won't know we're going and won't have time to plot anything."

Tonya bit her lip and nodded. "All right, if you think it's safe."

He thought it was; Tonya didn't seem so sure. He just hoped she didn't prove to be right.

Clay met them back at the ranch. Once again they gathered around the table. Seth's mother started putting together some drinks and snacks as soon as they sat down. Clay frowned as Seth related the incident in the grocery store. "I can pull some video footage, but if he had on a ball cap and wanted to avoid the cameras, we probably don't have any hope of seeing his face."

"But it might *not* have been him," Seth countered. "If it wasn't, he wouldn't care about the cameras and we could confirm that it wasn't Hank."

Clay nodded. "Very true. All right, I'll go by and speak to WC and see if I can get a couple of shots to show you."

"Thank you," Tonya said.

"Wait…hold up a second," Seth said. "I have another idea."

"What's that?" Clay asked.

Seth leaned forward. "We've already established that we're not sure who that guy was in the grocery store. Could have been no one. Or it could be that Hank's found Tonya somehow. We just don't know. We also don't know that he doesn't know where Tonya is staying. But what if he shows up tonight?"

Clay rubbed his chin. "I see what you're saying, little brother. I also see the wheels in your head spinning. What do you have in mind?"

"What if Tonya stays in your old cabin tonight and we stake out her motor home?"

Clay gave a slow nod while he let his gaze bounce back and forth between Tonya and Seth. "That might not be a bad idea."

"Of course it's not a bad one—I thought of it."

Clay smirked, then turned serious again. "All right, let's do it. I'll come stake out the motor home from dusk until two. I'll get Lance to take the other half of the night."

Tonya bit her lip but didn't protest.

Clay left and Seth reached across the table to grasp her fingers in his. "It's going to be all right."

"You keep saying that."

"Because I believe it and I want you to do the same."

She sighed. "I *want* to believe it."

"But?"

"I guess I'll have to see it first."

Seth's father stomped into the kitchen and chugged a bottle of water from the refrigerator. When he finished, he looked at Tonya. Then their linked hands. Seth didn't pull away and neither did Tonya.

"How'd you manage to fall off that bull, son?"

Seth gave a good-natured groan and dropped his head. "It just happened, Dad." He paused. "But you know, I still haven't gotten to take a look at that rope. I wonder if Jake can get it from the storage room where Mia put it."

"Why?"

Seth shrugged. "Just curious to look at it."

"Why?" This time his father's question was more forceful, his gaze more intense.

Seth took another swig of his tea. "Because I think it moved."

"Moved?"

"Slipped." He didn't want to go into more details in front of his mother, but his dad wasn't slow.

Ross lowered his glass, his eyes never leaving Seth. "Slipped how?"

"I don't know. That's why I need to lay eyes on it." Seth glanced at his mother, who seemed oblivious to the conversation as she gathered items she'd need for dinner from the pantry.

His father gave a short concerned nod, then looked at Tonya. "You like to ride?"

She smiled. "Of course."

"You know anything about taking care of horses?"

"Been doing it all my life."

Seth cleared his throat. "Dad, are you trying to rope Tonya into helping you with the horses?"

Ross flushed and shrugged. "Only if she wants to."

Tonya stood and pulled her hand from his. Seth mourned the loss. "I'd love to," she said.

"Wait a minute," Seth protested. "I didn't bring her here so you could put her to work."

His father opened his mouth. Before he could speak, Tonya said, "I don't mind, really. It'll take my mind off stuff."

"Then I'm coming, too." Seth stood and limped his way to the door to hold it open for her.

TEN

Tonya slipped past him and headed for the barn. The heat of the afternoon washed over her, but it couldn't stop the shiver that slipped up her spine.

What if it had been Hank in the grocery store? What if he'd been watching them and followed them out to the ranch? Were she and Seth's family now sitting ducks? No, it couldn't have been him. He'd have no way to find her.

But what if somehow it was?

Anger swept through her. This was not fair to Seth's family. It wasn't fair to her either, but…life wasn't fair. She got that. However, this was ridiculous. A four-year nightmare that had to end.

"Sorry about this," Seth said.

Jerked from her thoughts, she tucked her phone in her back pocket and blinked at him. "Why?"

"Putting you to work like you're some hired hand," he grumbled.

She gave him a small smile. "I don't mind. It's good to stay busy."

"All right, well, you're not doing it all by yourself. I'm not completely helpless." He handed her a pitchfork and she walked to the first stall.

She clicked to the horse, slipped the halter over him

and led him to the side, where she clipped a hook into the silver ring of the halter. "Just stay here, boy, while I get you all fixed up."

They worked in silence, Seth in one stall—favoring his left leg, she noticed—and she in another. Finally, she leaned the pitchfork against the wall and stepped into the restroom next to the office. She ran cold water and splashed it on her hot face. It felt good to be working with the animals. At least she didn't have to watch her back with them.

The barn was as familiar to her as the back of her hand. All barns smelled and felt the same, in her opinion. She'd taken note of the layout. An L-shaped building, it had forty stalls total—twenty stalls down one part and twenty down the other. Each row of stalls held ten on each side with a dirt floor and hay in between. In the main area, she'd seen the office and restrooms at one end, the horse bathing area at the other. Bales of hay rested neatly in the loft, waiting to be thrown down and fed to the horses. Outside, she had a clear mental picture of the trees, pasture and riding trails out behind the barn. It was a classy place for sure and she could see why Seth loved it.

"Seth? You in here, son?"

"Over here, Dad."

At the sound of the voices, Tonya came out of the bathroom in time to see Ross stepping out of the office, envelope in hand, looking all riled up. Seth set his pitchfork aside and faced his father. "What is it?"

"Mortgage payment. Thought your mom mailed it two weeks ago. Now I've got to get it there by Monday or they'll charge us a late fee." His jaw tightened. "We can't afford to throw money away like that." He threw his hands up. "But I can't find a stamp. Thought I had a whole roll of them in my desk." Tonya could hear the man's frustration.

"I've got a stamp in my trailer," Seth said. "Come on. We'll get it and run it down to the box." He looked back at Tonya. "I'll just be a few minutes."

She nodded and Ross followed Seth out of the barn. A simple trip to the mailbox at the end of the long drive could take a bit more than a few minutes. But it would give Seth some time with his father. Tonya turned back to the horse, stroked its neck, then simply stared at the opposite wall. The horse nudged her and she absently rubbed his ears as she took a moment to review her options. And came to the sad conclusion that they hadn't changed since the last time she'd considered them.

She could leave. Climb in her motor home and take off... Or she could stay and potentially put the Starke family at risk. Neither option sounded good to her.

Or she could call Grant. If she found a pay phone in town. Did they even have those anymore? Or she could borrow a cell phone. It might sound paranoid, but she had a feeling Hank had a way to monitor incoming calls to her family and would track down any call that came from out of town. Especially one with a Tennessee area code. He'd done it before; she felt sure he would do it again.

A door opened and shut and she stiffened. "Seth? Ross? Did you forget something?"

Silence answered her.

Her nerves tightened and she moved to grasp the pitchfork she'd discarded earlier. Her fingers curled around the wooden handle and she hefted it into a defensive position. She listened, ears tuned to her surroundings, seeking that one sound that didn't belong.

A shuffle, a shoe scraping the floor.

Her nose twitched. No cologne. But could the barn

smells cover it? Probably not. Then again, what if he just hadn't put any on?

She looked around, her pulse accelerating, heart thudding in her chest. She swallowed and moved toward the stall she'd just cleaned. One door was at the opposite end of the barn. The strange noises she'd heard were coming from the other part of the L-shaped building and she'd have to go toward them to get to the second door.

She wasn't near an exit or a window. She moved slowly, taking the pitchfork with her.

The footsteps drew closer. Lighter footsteps. Not heavy like a man's. Like Hank's. Tonya crouched in the rear of the stall, the business end of the pitchfork aimed toward the door. A pair of boots appeared in front of her.

A door opened, then slammed. "Tonya?"

Tonya stiffened at Julianna's voice. The boots turned and hurried in the opposite direction. Tonya lunged for the stall door and threw it open. Seth's mom walked toward her, a smile on her face and a plate of cookies in her hand. "Thought you might enjoy a treat."

"Did you see someone just now? Right outside this stall?"

Julianna frowned. "No. Why?"

A chill slithered up Tonya's spine. If it hadn't been Julianna, Ross, Seth—or even Hank—standing outside the stall door, who had it been?

Seth stepped back into the barn to find his mother and Tonya sitting on the feed bins eating oatmeal-and-chocolate-chip cookies. He stopped and stared and his heart gave a joyful thump in his chest. The barn was dim, most of the lights being left off until they were needed. But Tonya sat under one of the brighter lights, completely focused on what his mother was saying.

Never had she looked more beautiful to him than at

that very moment. He knew he'd always liked her, liked her smile, her compassion, her friendliness. He'd admired and respected her because of her skills and her exemplary work ethic. But seeing her sitting there with her hair tied up in a messy ponytail, dirt streaking her left cheek, sweat ringing her T-shirt at the armpits, he felt something else stir in his heart. Not just attraction, although that was definitely there, but more of an emotional connection. A desire to know everything there was to know about her—and to have the time to get to know it.

But what would she say if she knew? He supposed he'd suffered enough rejection in his life that if she only wanted to remain friends, he would survive. Maybe. The sharp bite of pain in the vicinity of his heart told him he was kidding himself. He wanted more than friendship with her.

He cleared his throat and the two women looked up. Tonya smiled at him and gestured to the plate. "We left you a couple."

"Thanks." He walked over and snagged three.

Tonya eyed his leg. "You're walking better."

"It's loosening up a bit."

"And the Motrin is helping?" his mother asked with a raised brow.

He flushed. "Definitely."

She grinned and Tonya gave a low chuckle. But the mirth didn't reach her eyes.

His mother stood and brushed off the seat of her jeans. "Guess I'll take the rest of these into the house so we have some for after supper tonight. I'll see you two later."

She slipped out the door and Tonya rose. "I like her."

"She likes you."

"How can you tell?"

"She made cookies and shared them with you."

Tonya laughed. A more sincere sound this time. "What's wrong?" he asked.

"Someone came in the barn after you and your dad left."

"Who?"

"I don't know. I called out your name and Ross's but no one answered. I could hear him getting closer and closer and I panicked. I couldn't get out the door, so I hid in the stall with the pitchfork. I saw a pair of boots stop in front of the stall door. Then your mother came in and the person left. Fast."

Seth frowned. "One of the hands who came in from the pasture?"

"I don't know. If so, why not answer me and let me know who was there?"

Seth narrowed his eyes. "And the person never said anything?"

"No, nothing."

"It could have been anyone, Tonya," he said quietly. "But it *is* weird the person didn't answer you. Maybe you called out too soon and he didn't hear you?"

"Maybe."

Seth was concerned, but not overly so. "We have a lot of people working today. Part-timers mostly, filling in with riding lessons and such, but I'll ask around."

"Okay." She gave a quiet sigh. "It was probably nothing. I'm being jumpy."

He exhaled roughly. "With good reason. We won't take any chances. We'll find out who was here."

"Thanks." She whispered the word and Seth moved closer.

He lifted a hand and cupped her cheek. "I won't let anything happen to you, Tonya."

"I know."

"You have chocolate on the side of your mouth." His gaze dropped to her lips.

She flushed. A bright red that he found endearing. And she didn't move away. Seth kept his eyes on hers and lowered his head until his lips touched hers. She gave a small sigh and leaned into the kiss. Seth kept it light but let it linger when she didn't protest. When he lifted his head, she opened her eyes. Hope and wonder stared back at him. Along with a little bit of trepidation? "Ah...do I need to apologize?"

She stepped back. "Um... I don't know."

"Are you telling me you don't feel the attraction between us?"

"I feel it," she whispered. "I just don't know if I want to."

Hurt slammed him. He kept his face expressionless, his reaction hidden. "Okay." He ran a hand through his hair. "Then I'll keep my distance."

"Seth—"

He held up a hand and let the hurt fade. "No, it's okay. It's not fair of me to add that to your already overflowing plate. You need to focus on staying safe and one step ahead of Newman."

"Yes, that's true, but—"

He covered her lips with a finger. "So. Want to help me finish up in here?"

She nodded and lifted a finger to wipe away the chocolate. He caught her hand. "I got it."

She flushed and he grinned. Tonya turned away, but not before he caught her slight smile. But it wasn't long before her smile faded. For the next half hour, they worked in silence. A tense silence. Not because of the kiss but because he knew she was wondering if Hank was out there.

Watching and waiting.

He had to admit he wondered the same.

Sunday morning, Tonya brushed her hair and washed her face. Last night had been a fun dinner with Seth's rather raucous family. It made her homesick for her own loud and obnoxious brothers. Brothers whom she loved and missed with an ache that never went away. And her mother… What she wouldn't give for a midnight chat, sitting on the end of the bed and drinking decaf coffee. And oh boy, did she ever have stuff to discuss with her mom. Like kissing Seth. Now, that had been amazing. And stomach twisting. And she wanted to do it again. What would her mother say to that?

"Don't let him get away, baby girl." Her mother's voice echoed in her head. Yeah, that was what she would say. And Tonya vowed to get through this hard time in order to have that conversation with her mother.

She swallowed against the tears and decided to be grateful that the night had passed with no sign of Hank— or anyone else. She didn't believe for one second that he'd given up and left the area, but she was beginning to believe he wasn't in Wrangler's Corner. Not yet, anyway.

But who'd been in the barn? her brain taunted.

Seth had asked around as promised and no one could figure out who had been there.

She sighed and put the finishing touches on some mascara even as Seth's reassurance that it was going to be all right kept looping through her mind. She hoped his proclamation didn't turn out to be famous last words.

"It *is* going to be all right," she whispered to the mirror. *Please let it be all right.* She washed and dried her hands and walked out of the cottage Clay used to call home.

Seth stood next to a bright red Ford truck. Police still

patrolled the area near the trees in the distance. Clay would make sure his family was protected. Tonya just felt bad there was a need.

She should have called Grant the minute she saw Hank and had him meet her somewhere, have his US marshal friend put her up in a safe house. Something—*anything*—except put Seth and his family in danger. Granted, nothing major had happened yet. She wanted to keep it that way. As did everyone else. Which was why Clay and Lance had decided to follow them to church.

"I still don't know that this is a good idea," she said as she approached. "We don't know who that man was in the grocery store and we don't know who was in the barn." She noticed Clay in one cruiser and the deputy in another. One would lead and the other would follow.

"Clay wouldn't let us go if he really believed Hank was here, but he's not taking any chances." His eyes flicked to her face. "You can't just stop living because he might be here."

"I don't know—"

"Clay will be behind us. He'll be watching to see if we're followed."

"And if we are?"

Stepping forward, he placed his hands on her shoulders. "He'll stop whoever follows us."

"But the people in the church… They'll be a target if I walk in there."

Seth shook his head. "Clay would never put those people at risk. He had someone sweep the church before the service. He'll have deputies posted throughout and he even has a couple of buddies who're snipers driving in from Nashville to be on top of buildings with rifles ready."

Tonya shivered. "Wow."

"Clay wants to catch this guy."

"Not as bad as I do," she muttered. Then drew in a deep breath and offered him a weary smile. "Do you want me to drive?"

"I can do it. It's my left leg that's hurt, not my right."

"Figured you'd say that." She climbed into the passenger seat and grimaced at the heat that slammed her.

"Why'd you figure that?" He slid in beside her and buckled his seat belt, cranked the engine and turned the air on high.

"You're a bit of a control freak."

"Who? Me?" He shot her a surprised look.

"Yep."

"Naw."

Clay knocked on the window and Seth rolled it down. "I'll be right behind you."

"I know."

His brother nodded. "All right, then, let's get going. I think a morning spent in prayer would be a good thing."

They started their trek down the mountain toward the town of Wrangler's Corner. Clay stayed with them, and within ten minutes Seth turned onto Main Street. "It's beautiful," she said.

Seth nodded. "It's a great place. I loved growing up here. Some of the teen years were harder than others, but riding bulls helped keep me out of a lot of trouble I might have been tempted to get into."

"I know what you mean." She paused. "You don't think I should run again, do you?"

"Nope."

A short and simple-enough response. "Aw, Seth, I really wish you wouldn't hold back on me. Tell me what you *really* think." He gave a snort of laughter that quickly died as he glanced in the rearview mirror. "What is it?" she asked.

"There's a car behind Clay that's been there for a while."

She looked in the side mirror and could see the black sedan trailing behind the police cruiser. "Do you think Clay noticed it?"

"Yes, I'm sure he's aware."

She kept watching until Seth turned onto one of the side streets. "Maybe you could call—" The car kept going and disappeared from view. "Never mind—it didn't follow us." She sighed. "I'm sorry."

"What?"

"I've made us all paranoid."

"You haven't—your stalker has. With good reason." He pulled into the parking lot of the small church. "And I don't know that I would call it paranoia. More like supercautious. Then again, if that translates to paranoid, then I'm all right with that."

"Good point."

Seth put the truck in Park but didn't cut the engine. He drew in a deep breath as though gathering the strength to say something. She released her seat belt and waited. From the corner of her eye, she saw Clay pull in beside them.

"Okay, I'm going to have to warn you," Seth finally said. He held an index finger up to indicate to Clay to give them a minute. The sheriff nodded.

"About...?" she asked.

"I grew up in this church," Seth said. "When we walk in together, there will be raised eyebrows and instant speculation."

Tonya understood exactly what he meant. She smiled and shook her head. "It's always that way. My home church would be the same way."

His breath whooshed out. "Then you're going to be all right with it?"

She shrugged. "People are people. They'll wonder and speculate and drive themselves crazy. I don't let stuff like that bother me."

He reached over and curled her fingers through his. "Good. I need to learn to be a bit more like you."

"Why? I've never noticed you letting what anyone thought influence you or bother you."

"Not on the outside, but on the inside…" He shrugged and looked away.

She blinked at the vulnerability he'd just let her see. A piece of himself that she instinctively knew he'd not revealed to others. "I'm sorry."

He swallowed and cleared his throat. "When I was injured and Glory walked out on me, it threw me. Big-time. I was embarrassed and hurt, yeah, but I couldn't believe that I was such a bad judge of character."

"We all make mistakes along those lines at some point in our lives. Look at me and Hank…"

He shook his head. "You saw through him pretty fast. Three dates and you knew you didn't want to be with him. I didn't see through Glory's shallowness until she had the power to break my heart."

"Which she did?"

He nodded. "To some extent."

"How do you feel about her now?"

He squeezed her fingers and shot her a somber smile. "I feel sorry for her because she's looking for happiness in the wrong places. She'll never be content with herself or who she is as long as she focuses on money and materialism and only being attached to 'winners.' She's not in a relationship for what she can do for the person she loves. She's in it to get what she can, milk it dry, then move on." He shook his head again. "I might have been like that at one time, but I'm not anymore."

"No," she said softly. "You're not like that at all."

"And neither are you, are you, Tonya?"

"No, I'm not."

He shot her another look and his lingering gaze made her cheeks flame. When he turned his eyes back to the church building, she bit her lip. He cleared his throat. "Did you know I wanted to ask you out the first time I saw you?"

She sucked in a sharp breath. "What?"

"Yep. Then Daniel came up and slapped me on the back and introduced you as his girlfriend." He winked. "I was heartbroken. Probably why I decided to go out with Glory."

"You're making that up."

He sobered. "Not the part about wanting to ask you out. But you were Daniel's and I wasn't about to do anything to mess up our friendship. So I walked away."

She tried to clear the emotion from her throat. "Daniel was a good man."

"Yeah, he was."

"But he cared too much about me. He loved me, but his love could be smothering. He wasn't like Hank, who is all about control, but Daniel drove me crazy sometimes with his need to keep me safe." Tears sprang to her eyes and she turned to look out the window. "And he died because of it." She sniffed and looked back at Seth. She pulled her hand from his. "Don't care about me too much, okay?"

ELEVEN

Seth sat through the service and struggled to keep his attention focused on the pastor's message. Tonya's words kept looping through his mind. *Don't care about me too much.* Could she really mean that? He shifted his leg and tried to find a more comfortable position. He supposed he understood her perspective on that statement. Daniel had died, had given his life because he'd loved Tonya. He hadn't meant to die, of course, but that didn't change facts.

And now Tonya was skittish about anyone getting close to her. He let his gaze stray to her pretty face. Oval features, some light makeup on her eyes, a dusting of blush on her cheeks. His heart thumped and he turned his gaze back to the pulpit. He'd had a hard time with God lately. With everything that had happened, Seth wanted to drown in a pot of self-pity, but he knew if he went there, he'd never be able to climb out. Instead he'd put God on the back burner and focused on physically healing. And winning.

And then Tonya had charged into his life and made him look at everything, including God, in a different light. It wasn't the Lord's fault Seth had allowed himself to be influenced by a woman he knew wasn't right for him. He had to take responsibility for that, not blame God.

He took another deep breath and let his gaze roam the church. As promised, deputies were in attendance. Some in uniform, some not. No one at the church seemed to notice the unusual number of deputies. Most of them were a part of the congregation anyway. Some showed up even when they were on duty since Sunday mornings tended to be the slowest day of the week when it came to crime in Wrangler's Corner.

But Seth noticed. When the service finally ended without incident, he breathed a sigh of relief. Maybe Hank had given up. Maybe they could relax their vigil just a little.

Maybe.

He and Tonya stepped out of the church and he gave a low groan when former Sunday-school teachers gathered around his mother and began their not-so-subtle questioning about the lady Seth had with him. He shook his head and cupped Tonya's elbow. "Let's go."

Clay caught his eye and nodded that he'd be right behind them.

"Clay?"

His mother's voice stopped his brother's trek toward the parking lot. "Yes?"

"Lunch will be on the table shortly. Do you and Sabrina and the children plan to join us?"

"Sure, that'd be great."

Seth saw Clay catch his wife's eye and felt his blood pressure drop a little. His brother wouldn't have told Sabrina to attend services if he thought there was a remote chance that Hank would show up.

He propelled Tonya to the car. "I'm starving—and restless. How about a ride after lunch?"

* * *

When she entered the barn, Seth was waiting on her, chilled bottles of water in his hands. He tossed her one.

"Thanks. Your mom is an amazing cook."

He shot her a smile. "Yep. And she loves to feed people."

"Clay's going back to the office, isn't he?" She swigged half the bottle.

"Sounds like that was his plan."

"Does he ever take time off?"

"Sure, but he's trying to find Hank Newman and it'll eat him until he's successful." He grabbed his hat from the table. "You ready to ride?"

"On a horse or in a vehicle?"

"A horse, of course." She glanced at his leg and he shrugged. "I'll be good. I'll rest the leg and let the horse do the work."

She finished the water and let out a long breath. "That sounds nice. Hot, but nice."

Seth nodded. "Why don't you get us two more waters from the fridge in the office and I'll let Dad know."

"Okay." Tonya watched him leave and shook her head at the way she just wanted to be near him. The thought of spending the rest of the day with him, riding horses and talking, appealed to her so much. *Too much.*

She moved to the barn office and grabbed the two bottles from the refrigerator. A piece of paper tacked to the corkboard caught her attention. She pulled it down even as she heard Seth's limping gait coming up behind her.

"Tell me about this. I saw the same flyer posted on the grocery-store door."

He stepped next to her to look over her shoulder. "Every year, our little town has a rodeo. It's a pretty big event around here. It's how I started bull riding," Seth said. "My brother Aaron is real involved in helping set up and taking care of any animals that might need it. You wait—in a couple of days, our barn is going to be full of rodeo gear." He grinned. "We get a lot of folks who come from out of town, too."

"I think I've heard of this. It's happening next weekend," she said.

"Yep."

"That's awesome. I can't believe I haven't paid more attention to this—or participated in it." Tonya kept reading. "It says they need riders and bullfighters."

"Most of the money goes to different charities," Seth told her. "The town just has to cover the costs to put it on, but there are so many donations that we usually raise forty or fifty thousand to divide between the charities chosen to receive the money."

Tonya stroked her chin.

"What are you thinking?" Seth asked curiously.

She lifted a shoulder. "I think it would be fun to be a part of something like that."

"So why don't you?"

She shot him a sad smile. "Today's Sunday. The rodeo starts Thursday. I don't know if I'll be alive on Thursday, much less able to commit to participating in a rodeo."

He scowled. "Don't talk that way. Of course you will."

"Let's pray you're right."

"I'll sign us up when we get back."

"Seth—"

"Why not? It's for a good cause and will give us something to look forward to."

She shrugged. "I'll think about it."

He studied her for a long moment, then walked into the office and sat down at the computer. She followed him and frowned. "What are you doing?"

"Signing us up." He logged in and pulled up the website.

"I said I'd think about it. You said you'd do it when you got back. I'm not finished thinking about it."

"You said you wanted to do it. If you think about it, you'll come up with a dozen reasons not to. Let's get signed up. If something comes up and you can't be there, I have a friend who can fill in."

"But—"

"Please?"

She sighed. He really wanted her to participate. She shrugged. "Okay, as long as you have a replacement."

He shot her a quick grin and finished the registration. When he stood, he tapped her nose. "You'll see—it'll be fun. And something to look forward to."

Understanding hit her. She'd gone so long living day by day, refusing to look to the future, scared to hope and plan, that to actually let him include her in something that was a week away left her feeling…weird. And in some strange way…hopeful.

She followed him out of the office. "Thanks."

He winked at her, then grabbed a saddle blanket from the peg on the wall and tossed it over the horse's back. He reached for the saddle next and winced when he stepped a little harder than he should have on his injured leg.

She reached for the next blanket to put on her horse and stopped when she caught his expression. "Seth, you're going to hurt yourself again."

"Naw. I've been saddling horses since before I could walk." She arched a brow and he shrugged. "Or somewhere about that age."

She sighed and shook her head as he placed the saddle on top of the blanket. Another wince.

Tonya couldn't stand it. "Let me finish that for you."

She moved to adjust the stirrup at the same time he bent down to tighten the girth. His cheek bumped her lips and she went still. Frozen. He pulled back and looked down into her eyes. She knew her face was a brilliant shade of red and thanked God that the barn was poorly lit. She cleared her throat and took a step back. "Ah, I think I'll just let you take care of that and I'll saddle my own horse. Over here. By the office."

A slow smile slid across his lips but he didn't say a word, just finished saddling the horse while favoring his left leg. Again silence reigned until he patted the horse's neck. "All done."

"Me too." She stuck her left foot in the stirrup and hauled herself up, swinging her leg over and catching the other stirrup with her right foot.

Seth had a bit of trouble getting in the saddle and finally succumbed to using a step stool. He shot her a warning look. "If you ever tell my brothers or the guys at the rodeo about this..."

From atop her horse, she held up a hand in the Boy Scout salute. "Never. I promise."

He grunted and she gave a soft laugh. He clicked to the paint and led the way out of the barn. Tonya followed him, admiring his form and the easy way he held himself in the saddle. Tonya realized that she felt almost relaxed for the first time in a long time. Hank might be coming after her, but this time she had people watching her back.

And she couldn't be more grateful. They rode out into the pasture for a few minutes before Seth pulled his horse to a stop and waited for her to come up beside him. "I have a question for you."

"What is it?"

"You said Hank Newman was the guy in the storage room where you were hiding."

She gave a shudder. "Yes."

"What did he look like?"

"Like the guy in the grocery store," she said. Then thought about it. "He looks different than when I knew him before. His hair was longer and he had a goatee and a mustache."

"That matches the man I talked with. And you recognized him?"

Tonya snorted. "I'd recognize him dressed in a full set of body armor." She bit her lip and looked out over the vast field of green. "I say that—and I've always thought that—but the truth is, when I first saw him again at the arena, it took me a minute because he did look different." Another shiver racked through her. "But then he caught my gaze and wouldn't look away. The longer he stared, the more uneasy I got. Then he gave me a little smile and I knew it was him." She shrugged. "And I ran. He must have seen me duck into the storage room and come after me."

"Hmm. I wonder if there were any video cameras."

"If there were, I'm sure the cops are looking at footage in order to see if they can figure out who planted that bomb in my cannon." She paused. "Would Clay be able to find out for you?"

"Sure."

"I'd like to analyze it myself. I want to see if the camera caught Hank in the hallway."

Seth pulled his phone from his pocket and pressed a number. "Clay, Tonya and I were just talking. Would you be able to get your hands on any video footage at the arena?" There was a brief pause. "Actually, we're specifically interested in the hallway near the dressing room and then the cameras focused on the arena when they were setting up for her stunt. Tonya wants to take a look and see if she can spot Hank Newman." He listened and she heard a snapping behind her. She turned and scanned the area. She and Seth had ridden to the edge of the woods to ride along the tree line. "Okay, thanks." He hung up. "My brother said he'd put the request in but didn't want you to hold your breath. He did say you might be able to go to Nashville to take a look."

She nodded, her mind still on the noise she'd heard. Was she being paranoid? Jumpy due to the circumstances she'd just run from?

Maybe.

"You ready to ride?"

"Sure." With another glance over her shoulder, she gave the horse a gentle nudge and they started walking. She stayed next to Seth. "Do you mind if I ask what happened with you and Glory after the accident?"

"She decided she wasn't interested in a bull rider with a broken leg—aka someone who was on the fast track to nowhere and empty pockets."

"Did she think you wouldn't heal?"

"I think she was afraid there'd be permanent damage, yes."

"That's crazy."

He shrugged. "I'm just glad I found out just how superficial she was before we walked down the aisle." He paused. "My mother didn't like her much. That should have been my first clue."

"Why not?"

He looked at her out of the corner of his eye. "She said she was shallow."

"I'm sorry."

"As I mentioned before, it hurt." They rode in silence a few more minutes with Tonya looking back every so often. He caught her gaze. "But it hasn't hurt so much lately."

Now he had her complete attention. Did he mean what she thought he meant? Or was she misreading the comment...? "I'm glad."

"Me too." Another pause. "Tell me about you and Daniel."

She winced and looked away. "I cared about him."

"Did you love him?"

She swallowed hard. "I loved him as a friend, yes. And maybe I even saw the potential to marry him one day. He was strong in his faith and had a gentle heart."

"But?"

She sighed. "But I wasn't ready to talk about marriage when he brought up the idea. I told him I wanted some time to think about it."

"Not that it's any of my business, but why?"

"I was really enjoying being free of Hank, free of my overprotective brothers. Just...free. I loved hanging out with Daniel, dating him and having a good time with him, but I wasn't ready for a commitment. Maybe that sounds as shallow as Glory."

"Of course not. Not everyone is ready for a commitment at the same time. That's why some people have long engagements." He paused and glanced at her from the corner of his eye. "But then Daniel died."

Tears clogged her throat. She tried clearing the lump, but it wouldn't go away. "You were there. You saw what happened. He died because he saw me in danger from the bull and didn't trust me enough to take care of myself." She set her jaw and pulled in a breath. "When he tried to help me, he got distracted and the bull caught him in the side with a horn. It knocked him to the ground. Daniel tried to roll while I worked to distract the bull. Others jumped into the arena to help, but it was too late."

A tear slid down her cheek and she swiped it away with a flick of her hand. "The bull's hoof came down on his head. Everyone was in the ring trying to get that bull away from Daniel, but…" Her words trailed away and were followed by more tears. "I'm sorry. I need to walk a minute."

In one smooth move, she slid off the horse and started heading down the trail. A loud crack sounded and bark flew from the tree in front of Seth's horse's head.

TWELVE

Seth dived for the ground. Another bullet spit up the dirt in front of him. "Tonya!" Fear coursed through him as his leg protested the harsh treatment. But that was his last worry. Right now he just wanted to avoid a bullet and make sure Tonya was safe.

"I'm okay," she called. "We need to get in the woods behind a tree!"

He rolled and found her standing beside him, hand out. "Are you crazy? Go!" His heart thudded as he grasped her hand and let her help haul him to his feet. Together they stumbled into the protection of the trees. Underbrush crunched beneath his feet. His leg screamed at him and he limped to crouch behind the largest trunk he could see. He pulled Tonya down with him.

"You have your phone?"

"Yes." She already had it pressed to her ear. She gave information to the dispatcher in a breathless whisper while he glanced around the trunk of the tree trying to get a location on the shooter. He couldn't wrap his mind around the fact that this was happening. Just six months ago his family had been held hostage and almost killed, and now this. He had to get to the rifle in his saddle's scabbard. The idea of aiming it at a human made his stomach turn.

He glanced at Tonya's scared white face and tightened his jaw. He'd do what he had to do to protect Tonya and himself. Another peek around the trunk of the tree and he spotted movement to their left. Headed straight toward them. He grabbed the phone and Tonya started to say something. He held a finger to his lips and nodded in the direction he'd seen the figure.

She went silent but held the phone so it wouldn't disconnect. He gripped her hand and prayed help would arrive fast. There was no way he could move quickly or quietly.

But the approaching figure indicated Seth was going to have to try or die where he sat.

Tonya knew help was on the way, but that didn't mean they'd get there in time. The dispatcher had told her that she'd relay the emergency to Clay and the other deputies on duty. She'd heard the last shot and demanded to know if they were all right. Before she could answer, Seth had made her stop talking.

And now they were being stalked. Hunted like prey. Nausea churned, but she was going to have to ignore it and do something. She could probably outrun Hank by herself, find a way to hide and wait him out. But she wouldn't leave Seth to the man's murderous intent. She glanced in Hank's direction. He'd moved a little to their right. She leaned in to press her lips against Seth's ear. "What do you want to do?"

She turned her head to keep an eye on Hank's moving form and Seth mimicked her. "It's going to take too long for help to get here. I need to get the rifle from the scabbard."

"Or if we could get on the horses, we could ride out of here."

His frustration with his inability to move as he was used to was obvious. A muscle jumped in his jaw and his narrowed eyes tracked Hank. Fortunately, Hank continued a search that led him away from where they huddled, but he wasn't far enough away to allow them movement or any real noise. She squinted. At least, she thought it was Hank. The ski mask hid any features, but the build was right. Maybe?

"Just sit tight," Seth whispered. "Let's see what he's going to do."

"Or I can go get the rifle."

That muscle in his jaw bounced harder. His hand squeezed tighter. Tonya flexed her fingers and he loosened his grip. She pulled her hand from his and moved, silent, like a shadow, around to the other side of the tree trunk. If Hank came their way, he'd see Seth but not her. She reached around and gripped his fingers to give a tug.

He tucked his good leg under him and rose. When he took a step, a branch snapped. Seth froze. Tonya flicked a look around the trunk at Hank. He, too, had stilled, his head cocked.

Seth remained rigid. She could see her stalker but knew he didn't see them. Not yet. But if he moved a little to the right, he might. She kept her fingers wrapped around Seth's and he slid around beside her. His pale face and clenched jaw spoke of his pain. But he didn't make a sound. Sweat dripped from his brow and Tonya knew her face was wet, as well. The humidity pressed in thick and hot. That mask had to be sweltering. The black-gloved left hand gripped the weapon.

"Stay here," she hissed. "I'll get the rifle."

"The horses may not even still be there."

She could barely hear him but caught enough of his quiet words to understand. "I know, but we don't have a choice."

They were on a remote part of the ranch. Even when the police arrived at the ranch house, they'd still have to figure out where she and Seth were. She glanced at the phone. The dispatcher was still with her. Tonya lifted the phone to her ear. "Where are they?" she whispered.

"One mile away."

Tonya risked a look at Hank. He'd moved closer but had his back to them. Right now he was stopped, listening, turning one way, then the next.

Tonya pressed the phone into Seth's hand and motioned toward the horses. He frowned and shook his head. She frowned back and set her jaw. It was because of her that he was in this danger; it was up to her to get him out of it. "I have to. It's our only hope." She barely breathed the words, but he understood and after a brief hesitation gave a short nod.

"You're right." A look she couldn't decipher crossed his face. "If he comes this way, I'll be able to buy you enough time to get on the horse and get away. Just be careful." He squeezed her hand and gave her a look of such profound concern she swallowed hard. She read the silent message and touched his cheek. She appreciated his willingness to sacrifice himself, but as far as she was concerned, that wasn't an option. They were both getting away. She turned and studied the area she'd have to navigate before she'd reach the horses.

She darted to the next tree and slid behind it. She glanced back. Hank didn't turn her way, so she dashed to the next and the next. Finally, she was at the edge where the trees ended and the open pasture began. The horses had moved, spooked at the shooting, no doubt, but now grazed about twenty yards away.

Tonya looked back to see movement just behind her. She wouldn't have thought it possible, but her heart thundered even harder in her chest. Then she caught sight of Seth and her knees wobbled for a moment. He broke through the tree line, limping, face ashen, but waved at her to go.

Her gaze immediately went behind him, but there was no sign of Hank. Tonya spun and started her approach to the horses. Thankfully, with the reins spilling on the ground, they didn't protest too much when she pulled their noses from the grass and led them toward Seth, who now limped as fast as he could in her direction.

A shot cracked the air and she gasped as a bullet spit up the dirt in front of her. She spun around to the other side of the horse for protection, praying the man wouldn't shoot the animal to get at her.

Seth reached the horse, yanked the rifle from the scabbard and dropped to the ground with a grunt. He lifted the weapon to his shoulder and looked down the scope. But didn't fire. Tonya dropped beside him. Another bullet whizzed over her head and she dropped her face into her palms. "Cover your ears," he commanded. She did and Seth's rifle snapped back a reply to Hank's fire. The horses shied and shifted but didn't run.

The world fell silent. They waited. Thirty seconds. One minute. Two. Five. Seth stood using the horse as a shield. Nothing happened.

"I think he's gone. If not, we need to get out of here while he's not shooting." He grasped the reins and moved around to the right side of the horse to mount with his good leg. He hauled himself into the saddle with a pained grunt and looked at her. "Should have done that the first time."

Tonya bolted onto the back of her horse and they didn't waste any time pulling the horses around and heading off at a gallop toward the ranch. Tonya breathed a prayer of thanks for their deliverance from the danger once again. As they crested the first hill, she spotted two vehicles headed their way. Seth pulled his horse to a stop and she let her horse step up next to him. "Is that the cops?"

"That's them. They had to stop and get vehicles that could navigate this terrain. Their police cruisers would have gotten torn up trying to drive over this land."

One of the reasons they'd been so long in getting there. They waited for the vehicles to approach. "I thought you were going to wait on me to get the rifle," she said.

"I was, but he started walking away from me about thirty seconds after you left. I waited for him to disappear through the trees and decided to make my move. Guess I made too much noise and he heard me and came after us." Seth's horse shied away as the vehicle in the lead pulled to a stop next to them.

Clay rolled his window down. "Are you all right?"

"We're alive. Shooter's still out there." Seth jerked his thumb toward the forested area they'd just escaped from. Clay used the radio attached to his shoulder to give his deputies an update.

"Did you recognize him?"

"He had a mask on," Tonya said, "but I've no doubt he was Hank Newman. I think it's safe to assume the man at the grocery store was Hank, too."

"I've got a deputy at the house. Y'all get back there and stay put. I'll give you an update as soon as I have one."

Clay and the others took off. Tonya looked at Seth, whose tight jaw and narrowed eyes said he wanted to join in the search. Instead he gave a slight shake of his head and clicked to his horse. The animal gladly headed toward the barn.

As they approached, she could see the police cruiser parked under the tree in between the barn and the main house. Seth rode his horse into the barn and she followed. Once inside, the officer joined them. "Clay radioed that you were on the way in. It's been quiet since I've been here."

"Good," Seth said. "Thanks, Ronnie."

"Sure thing. Hate that you all are having trouble again."

"Yeah, me too."

As she dismounted and pulled the saddle from the animal, Ronnie stepped just outside the door to keep watch. Tonya brushed the horse down and her mind spun while Seth worked beside her. Leave? Or stay?

"You're not running again," he said gruffly.

"What do you mean?"

"I can see your brain working." He led his horse to the side of the stall, where he clipped the lead rope to a hook screwed into the wood.

"It's working, all right. I can't figure out how he knew to come out here, how to find me."

Seth shook his head. "I don't know either. Clay followed us practically all the way to the house. He said no one tailed us and I believe him. Did you tell anyone you were coming with me?"

"No."

He brushed the horse down and sprayed him with fly repellent. "Okay, then we're missing something."

"Unfortunately, I can't think what it might be." Tears gathered behind her eyes and she looked away. Not fast enough apparently. He snagged her arm and pulled her into a sweet embrace. She inhaled the scent of sweat and that musky cologne she'd grown to love.

"Just keep trusting me, Tonya. I'm here for you and I'm going to keep you safe," he whispered in her ear.

"I know," she whispered back. Then lifted her head to look him in the eyes. "And I'm really glad you are." Guilt nearly smothered her. "But the danger I've brought into your life, your family's lives, I—" She shook her head. "I'm so sorry. But I'm glad you're with me. I can't say I'm not."

"Tonya, I want to—"

She pressed her finger against his lips. "Later, Seth. When all of this is over."

He hesitated, his struggle between wanting to speak his mind and accede to her wishes clear. He finally nodded.

She followed out of the barn, moving slow in order to stay next to him. Ronnie brought up the rear.

As they moved close to the house, Seth's mother unlocked and opened the kitchen door, her face pinched and worried.

Ronnie gestured to his car. "I'll be out there, watching. I might drive around the house every so often, so if you don't see me sitting there, just give me a minute or two to get back."

"Thanks again."

The deputy left.

"What happened out there?" his mother demanded. "Clay stopped long enough to tell me to lock the doors, get my rifle and stay put."

Seth sighed and told her what had happened. Afterward Tonya ran a hand through her disheveled hair.

"Larry fixed my motor home. I'll leave first thing in the morning," she said softly.

"Leave?" Julianna looked at her, a frown creasing her forehead. "You're not leaving just because you're in danger. You need to stay here so we can watch out for you."

"It's not just me. It's you and your family, too." She blew out a frustrated breath. First Seth refused to hear of her leaving, and now his mother?

The woman waved a dismissing hand. "We've lived through it before. They'll catch him." She turned back to finish her lunch preparations. "The doors are locked and we'll put our ranch hands on alert to take precautions. Clay will send some of the deputies out here more often. We won't be stupid, but we won't be bullied either."

Tonya lifted a brow at Seth and he shrugged even as he scowled. He tried to pace but couldn't because of his bum leg, so he grabbed the rifle and went to lean against the wall beside the window. The tension in his shoulders made her want to weep. She'd brought this to them.

She controlled her raging emotions and went to the sink. She washed her hands and turned to Seth's mother. "What can I do to help?"

His mother gave her a quick hug. "You're a dear, but I think I've got it." Then she looked in Tonya's eyes and whatever she saw made her pause. "Actually, the glasses are in that cabinet next to the refrigerator. If you'll put some ice in them, that'll help."

Relieved to have something to do, Tonya got to work. As she filled the last glass, the door opened and Seth's brother stepped inside.

Tonya's gaze flew to Clay's and the grim look on the sheriff's face didn't reassure her. "He got away," she said.

"He got away."

THIRTEEN

Seth's fingers curled against his palms. He wanted to hit something. Preferably Hank Newman's face. Clay pulled out a chair and took a seat. Seth and Tonya did, too. "Hi, Mom," Clay said.

"Hello, dear. Tea?"

"Please. A big glass, thanks. Where's Dad?"

"Out in the barn cleaning out two empty stalls. He's got a fellow who wants to board his horses and is bringing them by later tonight. Aaron promised to drop by and give them a checkup, so I'm going to do a pot roast. Bring Sabrina and the kids around six."

She poured three glasses of tea and set them on the table in front of Clay, Seth and Tonya. After a long swig, Clay placed the glass on the coaster. "That sounds good— thank you. We'll be here." He looked at Tonya. "Okay, here's the latest…" He pulled his phone from his pocket and tapped the screen. "I got a report on your guy Hank Newman."

"Tell me." She leaned forward. Seth shifted beside her and placed his arm across the back of her chair.

"Hank's been out of prison for a while, as you know. But a couple of weeks ago he showed up at a woman's house and roughed her up pretty good." He frowned.

"Apparently they'd been an item shortly after he started his job with his brother. She called the police after the altercation took place, but Hank was gone by the time they got there. Hank showed up for work the next day, and when the police questioned him, he had his story ready. They let it go."

"Shocker," Tonya muttered. Seth silently agreed. He knew the police sometimes had their hands tied when it came to "he said" and "she said" testimony.

Clay nodded. "He supposedly took off for the conference, but we double-checked again, and while his badge and packet were picked up, no one can actually say that they've seen him since. So...as of this moment, no one knows where he is—"

Tonya snorted. "I do. He's just told us he's in Wrangler's Corner."

Clay nodded again. "I believe you. We have a crime scene unit from Nashville out there scouring the woods, looking for bullet casings. We found one. When we catch Hank and examine his weapon, if it matches, he's going down for attempted murder."

Tonya stood. "I just don't understand how he found us so fast." She looked at Seth then Clay. "You followed us. No one else did. And yet two days later, Hank Newman is shooting at us."

"Someone told him where to find you," Seth said.

"We talked about that, but I still don't know who it could have been." She paused and rubbed her forehead.

"The fact that this guy has come onto a property he's not familiar with and tried to shoot you..." Clay shrugged. "That tells me a lot about his personality."

"It's strange," Tonya said.

"What?" Seth asked.

"That's just *not* his personality. It's not like Hank to take that kind of risk."

"Really," Clay said, his eyes glinting with interest. "What would you have expected him to do?"

"Well, for starters, he would scope the place out for a couple of days, get routines, note who was on the ranch and where and at what time. For him to come out here without doing that is…strange." Her agitation was almost a physical thing. Seth grasped her hand and squeezed. She relaxed a fraction. "I mean, he'd probably been following me for the last couple of rodeos before he let me know he was there. So for him to do anything not planned—" She sighed. "It's just not like him."

Clay lifted a brow. "Well, then it might not *be* him." He shifted and took another swig of his tea. "I think we're looking at this wrong. I want to know how Hank found you here, yes—if it's him—but what I really want to know is how he found you in the first place. How did he know to show up at the rodeo?"

Tonya sat back down, but Seth could still feel the tension emanating from her. "I've been racking my brain trying to figure that out, but I honestly don't know."

"I'm telling you, someone *had* to tell him," Seth insisted.

"All right." Clay nodded. "Then who?" His question was directed at Tonya. "Go through the list of people who knew you were working the rodeo that Hank would have access to."

She bit her lip. "No one." She paused. "Except Grant, my brother, and maybe the US marshal who helped me run. Neither one of them would tell Hank where I was."

Seth heard the question at the end of her sentence. "You don't sound so sure."

"I… I'm sure." She sighed and rubbed her eyes. "I mean maybe."

"Come on, Tonya," Clay pushed, his tone intense and just a bit brusque. "I want to help you, but I need all the facts."

"The only family member who might be coerced—um…bribed—to tell Hank where I am is my brother Jacob, but he wouldn't have any idea where I was. Unless Grant told him, and I don't see that happening."

"Grant could have the information somewhere and Jacob found it—or was bribed to find it," Seth interjected. "But why him?"

"He has…*had*…a drug problem. Hank knew this because it was all happening when he and I first went out. Jacob showed up at my dorm room demanding money for a hit. I had a hard time getting rid of him, but he finally left after I threatened to call security. Hank was there for the show." Shame flashed in her eyes for a brief moment. Then her jaw jutted out. "I just can't believe that Jacob would do that, but then again, he did a lot of things during those dark days that I wouldn't have believed him capable of."

"Junkies are capable of just about anything," Clay said grimly. His phone beeped, but he didn't look away from her.

"Yeah," she whispered. "But he's my brother and I love him. It's hard to acknowledge those things." She sniffed and wiped away a stray tear. "But truly, I don't think he would even know how to find me. Grant's the one who got me all of my documents and did the name change. He wouldn't even tell my mother where I was, so I'm sure he didn't tell Jacob."

"Well, someone figured it out because it sounds like Hank had to have had help finding you. If that's the case,

Jacob seems a reasonable suspect." Seth reached over and clasped her hand and looked at Clay. "So what's next?"

"I'm posting more security around the ranch. The workers have been warned about stopping strangers. I'm also going to pass Hank's picture around town and tell people to stay on the lookout for him and report him if they see him. It's a small town. If he's here, someone will spot him." He leaned back in his chair, fingers steepled in front of him. "I'll also do a discreet search into Jacob's bank accounts and see if he's deposited any large amounts of cash lately."

Seth sighed. "All right." He looked at Tonya. "So you're going to be here for the rodeo. Have you thought about it long enough?"

"The rodeo?" Clay asked, eyeing him curiously. "The one here in Wrangler's Corner next weekend?"

"That's the one."

Clay's frown deepened. "You thinking of riding?"

"Maybe. And I'm trying to talk Tonya into bull-fighting for it. We don't have another rodeo until after that one. And since I've ridden in the WC Rodeo for the last ten years, no reason I should miss this one."

"No reason except riding too soon with an injured leg," Clay scoffed.

Seth rolled his eyes. His brother's phone beeped again.

Ignoring Seth, Clay finally glanced down at his phone. Tapped the screen. "Well, well, I may have the video footage from the rodeo arena sometime tomorrow afternoon."

"Wow. That was quick!" Tonya said. "How'd you manage that?"

Clay shrugged. "I worked in Nashville and have some good friends there. One of them is willing to share. And besides, if it turns out Hank's the one who put the bomb in that cannon, we'll be releasing footage of the video to the press so we can get the public looking for this guy."

Seth nodded. Tonya bit her lip and let her gaze dart back and forth between him and Clay. Seth scooted closer and gently brushed his knuckles against her cheek. "Are you up to watching some video footage tomorrow?"

She gave a slow nod. "I'm up to it."

"Good. It's going to be all right."

She gave another nod, but Seth couldn't tell if she believed him or not. He thought if he had to vote, he'd go with "not."

FOURTEEN

Monday afternoon, when they pulled into the parking lot of the police station, Tonya blew out a relieved breath. Finally, they were going to get some answers. She'd stayed awake almost all night, fearful that Hank would try to break into her trailer, but there'd been no sign of him.

That worried her even more. It meant he was thinking and planning.

She climbed out of the truck as Seth was rounding the bumper. He held the door for her and shut it when she was clear. Seth snagged her fingers and she felt the tension running through him. "It's going to be all right," he whispered.

"Yes…" She gazed up at him, his good looks striking her extra hard. But more than that, his compassion and caring…and determination to keep her safe.

"You still don't believe me, do you?"

"I'm reserving judgment," she hedged.

He glanced around and she followed his gaze. Clay and Ronnie were right behind them.

They entered the building and Tonya felt her shoulders relax. Every time she managed to get from one place to another without someone shooting at her or trying to grab her, it was a relief.

A sleepy Monday afternoon in Wrangler's Corner

most likely didn't elicit much excitement, so when she entered, all eyes turned on her with raised brows and speculation. Much like her reception at the church.

Clay led them to the back room without a word to the receptionist or the other two deputies sharing an office just off the entrance.

Seth's brother opened the door to a nice-sized conference room and Tonya saw Lance seated at the table, his eyes glued to a computer screen.

"Lance, you find anything worth watching yet?" Clay asked.

Lance glanced up. His blue eyes landed on her for a brief moment, then moved to Seth and Clay. He nodded. "Hey, you got here just in time." He was a big man and filled out his uniform in a way that most people might find intimidating, but Tonya thought she could see a hint of sadness in his eyes. He motioned them closer, picked up a remote and brought the images on the computer into mega size thanks to the large screen on the wall. "I decided to start going through the footage based on the date and time of the incidents you described to try and save us all some time. I'll show you the clips and you can tell us what you think. Have a seat." He motioned to two chairs at his left.

Tonya settled into one. Seth pulled one of the chairs from the stack against the wall and placed it next to the vacant chair beside Tonya. He dropped into the chair beside her and propped his leg up on the other. Clay took a seat near Lance at the conference table.

The deputy pressed Play and Tonya kept her gaze on the screen. People moved in the hallway outside her dressing room. A man in a black T-shirt and khaki pants walked past her door. "I can't see his face."

"I know," Lance said. "Just wait a second." He clicked

a few more keys on the computer and another clip came up. "This is the area outside the storage room where you said you hid." The video started and she gasped when she saw herself bolt into view, open the door and disappear. Only a few seconds later, the man in a black T-shirt and khaki pants followed, his gaze moving back and forth, scanning the hall and the area around him. She clearly saw his face a split second before he twisted the knob, stepped inside the room and shut the door.

"That's him. That's Hank."

"But that's not all. Look at this." Lance clicked a few more keys and brought up the arena. The crowd milled. A lot of the seats were still empty. A figure moved toward the cannon, which was already set up.

The ball cap hid the man's features and he kept his head lowered, but the goatee flashed with one turn of his head. "He has on a staff uniform," she breathed. "That's why he was able to move around so easy."

"He didn't have that on when he went into the storage room," Seth said, eyes narrowed.

"So he changed before he worked on the cannon."

Seth ran a hand over his jaw and stared again. "Can you freeze the part that shows the uniform, then go back to the initial video and freeze it when I tell you?"

"Sure." Lance clicked the appropriate keys.

"Now bring the two pictures up beside each other."

Again Lance complied.

"Looks like the pants are the same and the black T-shirt possibly, but he has the gray staff shirt pulled on over it in this picture here," Seth said, pointing to the image. "And a name badge with a lanyard."

"So he could go out into the arena without anyone stopping him," Tonya mused. "That's when he planted the bomb. But where did he get the shirt?"

"Good question." Clay pulled a notebook and pen from his pocket. "I'll see if anyone reported a missing staff shirt."

"And I'll put in a request to the FBI and see if they can use their equipment to enhance the badge and get a name," Lance said.

"What about the video footage from the grocery store?" Tonya asked.

"I couldn't get any," Clay said. "I talked to the owner and the camera hasn't been working for about a year now."

Tonya sighed. Another headache was starting to form. "All right, so what now?"

Seth leaned toward her, taking her chin in a gentle grip. "We make sure you stay safe."

"Seth's right, Tonya," Clay said. "That's our top priority." He checked his phone. "I asked to see the report on the bomb at the arena and my buddy came through."

"What's it say?" Seth asked, releasing her and shifting his gaze to his brother.

"It was triggered to blow as soon as the mechanism was released to shoot her out of the cannon."

"Meaning she never would have made it out of the cannon alive. It would have exploded with her in it."

"Yes."

Tonya shuddered and felt slightly sick. "I'm so tired of Hank Newman and the control he has over me!"

"Then we need to take that control away from him," Seth said.

She frowned and glanced from man to man until she finally settled back on Clay. "How do you propose to do that?"

"We set another trap."

It was Seth's turn to frown. "What kind of trap?" he asked. "And what would you use as bait? Because it's *not* going to be Tonya." He stood, ignoring the ache in his leg.

Clay held up a hand. "Sit down, little brother. I'm not

sure of all the details yet. Let me see if I can come up with a plan..." His eyes narrowed and his jaw tightened. The silence stretched until he finally said, "Yes, this trap will need bait and I'll need more officers than I have now, so I'll have to contact the department in Nashville, where I have some friends who would be willing to lend a hand." He shook his head. "You guys need to lie low until we get this settled."

"Wait a minute," Seth said. "Church yesterday. What was that? A trap, too?"

Clay held up a hand again. "No, no, not at all. That was a show of force. I wanted Hank to see that he wasn't intimidating anyone—that we were here, we knew about him and we're ready for him. If he was watching, he got the message."

"What if he had tried something? Like opening fire on the congregation or throwing a bomb into the church or—?"

Clay shook his head. "Maybe there was a slight risk to that, but I don't think so."

"You don't *think* so? Our parents were there!"

Clay stared at him and Seth snapped his lips shut. He looked at Lance, who had his arms crossed, expression shuttered. Tonya's cheeks had darkened a deep red and her brows were drawn tight.

Clay narrowed his eyes. "I know that. And if I truly thought that any of our loved ones were in danger, I wouldn't have done it, but I've had some training, Seth."

"Training in what?" If his leg hadn't been aching, he'd have gotten up and paced to work off his anger and frustration toward his brother.

"Profiling, little brother, profiling."

Seth closed his eyes and drew in a deep breath. Tonya still hadn't said a word. "Okay. Explain. Please."

Clay nodded. "Tonya, from your previous description of Hank, I suspect that he's a sociopathic narcissist. He thinks the world revolves around him. He has no regard for others or even authority, but he can be charming and convince everyone he's Mr. Nice Guy."

"Yes, that's him," Tonya whispered.

"These types of men don't usually form attachments, but they do like control. They also don't like rejection."

"Which is why he fixated on me. I rejected him."

"Yes, most likely," Clay replied. "He wasn't used to that, had probably never had to deal with it. He's the baby in his family and, according to my report, was doted on and spoiled."

She sighed and massaged her forehead. "But what about the fact that he shot at us in the woods? That was really out of character."

Again Clay nodded. "That makes me wonder, but there's nothing that says psychopaths can't deviate from the textbook definition."

"So there *could* have been some risk at the church." Seth glared at his brother.

Clay sighed and exchanged a glance with Lance, who shrugged. "I suppose, but we had security so tight I believe the risk was minimal." He spread his hands. "And nothing happened."

Tonya's lower lip trembled and Seth thought he saw a sheen of tears in her eyes. He ached to make this nightmare go away for her. He gripped her fingers. "It's—"

"I know—'it's going to be all right.'" She flashed him a tremulous smile and Seth didn't take offense at her interruption. He smiled back.

"Now, the fact that your guy hasn't made a move since the shooting tells me he's probably regrouping, lying low, assessing, planning, thinking," Lance said. "Clay and

I've discussed this and we've had deputies asking around town about any new strangers or tourists."

Seth frowned.

"Unfortunately," Clay said, "it's summer and the rodeo next week is bringing people in by the busload. We've also been showing his picture to the locals and telling them to call if they see this guy. Nothing so far."

Tonya nodded. "All right, then. What kind of trap did you have in mind?"

"It comes down to this... If Hank can't have you... then he wants to watch you die."

She drew in a sharp breath and the color leached out of her face.

"Clay!" Seth shot his brother a lethal look. Even Lance had a frown on his face as he stared at his boss.

"Sorry, maybe I could have worded that better." Clay held up a hand. "All I meant is the previous attempts on your life have been orchestrated in ways that would allow him to either physically kill you with his hands—by strangulation or shooting you—or in ways that are going to allow him to watch...i.e., the bomb in the cannon." His lips thinned. "Do I think he cares if another innocent person gets hurt in the process? No. But he's not going to do anything unless he can participate or actually see you die."

Tonya leaned back and Seth watched her process Clay's chilling words. She gave a slow nod, her face still pale. "You're right."

"So now we need a plan," Seth said. "And this time I want to know the details."

Clay nodded, a hesitant nod, but at least he agreed. He stood. "Come on. I'll follow you two back to the ranch. I've got a couple of deputies who are patrolling it every couple of hours."

"Have you gotten any information back about my brother?" Tonya asked. She bit her lip when Clay nodded once again and felt guilt swamp her for not stating she didn't want to know what he found. Then again, if he was innocent, the facts would defend him. If he was guilty...

Clay glanced at her as he sat back down. "That was the next thing on my agenda to talk to you about. I spoke to your older brother Grant. Told him what was going on."

Tonya gasped in surprised relief. "You did?"

"Yes."

"And Jacob?"

"Looks like he's cleaned up his act."

A tear leaked down her cheek. "I'm so glad," she whispered.

"He said there's no way Jacob could know where you were. Grant said he didn't have any kind of record of it in any computer or hard-copy file. Any information related to Tonya Lewis was erased so as not to leave a trail. And he said he wants to see you."

"I want to see him, too." She drew in a ragged breath. "Then it wasn't Jacob who led Hank to me."

"No, doesn't look like it. It's got to be someone else."

Tonya massaged her temples. "This is crazy. There *is* no one else."

"Except the US marshal," Seth reminded her. "She's the one who accessed the documents in the first place."

Tonya shook her head. "She wouldn't give me away. And besides, I've moved around so much she would have no idea where to find me. And before you ask, she doesn't have my phone number to trace it. Only Grant does."

Clay shrugged. "What about your friends at the rodeo? The one you seemed to be close to? Mia?"

Tonya frowned. "Mia knows about Hank. I told her

over a year ago along with some of the other ladies who were sitting at the table."

"What ladies?"

"A couple of barrel racers, Kelly and Sharon. Kelly was in an abusive relationship and wasn't sure what to do. I told her my story to convince her getting out was definitely the way to go but to be aware of stalker behavior. I told her what to look for, but I never gave Hank's name, though."

"You're sure?" Clay asked.

She narrowed her eyes. "I'm sure. I avoided any mention of him. When I say his name, it makes the memories just harder to deal with. I'd rather he remain nameless." She went still and tilted her head. "Glory was there."

Seth snapped to attention. "What?"

"She came up to speak to Sharon about borrowing a costume for the ride the next day and was there for the rest of the conversation."

Clay's phone pinged and he looked at it. For several moments silence echoed through the room while he read whatever it was that had him so riveted. He looked up. "Well, that's interesting."

"What?" Seth asked.

"It seems that Hank Newman had ten thousand dollars in cash deposited to his checking account five days ago."

FIFTEEN

Tonya shook her head and sighed. "Okay, so someone paid him to come after me? That doesn't make any sense. No one paid him anything four years ago to attack me. Who would pay him—?" She ran a hand through her hair. "Argh! Nothing makes sense anymore."

"So what's changed between then and now?" Clay asked.

"Nothing." She stood and walked to the nearest window and looked out. "Nothing."

Seth rubbed his eyes. "Okay, wait a minute. You said you found your favorite chocolates on your motor-home steps every Christmas."

"Yes."

"What if someone followed Grant?"

She shook her head. "That's only at Christmas."

"But you're always in the same place every Christmas."

She sank back onto the chair. "At the finals. In Las Vegas."

"Grant would know that."

"Of course he would." She frowned. "But if Hank followed Grant back in December, why wait six months to start terrorizing me again?"

Seth pursed his lips and looked at Clay. "Good question."

"Did you two talk about coming to Wrangler's Corner around anyone at the rodeo?"

Seth shook his head. "No, no one."

Clay stood. "All right. Let's get you two back to the ranch." Clay's phone rang. "Let me get that."

Tonya and Seth slipped out the door and Lance followed them. They stood in the hall and waited for Clay to finish his call. "Thanks for your help, Lance."

"Of course. Anytime." He glanced at Seth's leg. "I heard you signed up to ride on Thursday night."

"Yep."

"You up for it?"

"I'm always up for it."

Lance turned to Tonya. "Saw you on the lineup, too."

She gave him a tight smile. "Yes."

"Think that's a good idea?"

She lifted a brow at Seth. "*He* seems to think this is all going to be cleared up by then."

"Sure hope he's right."

Tonya nodded. "I do, too. Don't worry—if it's not, I won't be there. I won't put anyone in danger."

"Hey, guys?" Clay stepped from the conference room and shut the door behind him. "That was one of my detective buddies in Nashville. He called to let me know that one of the workers from the rodeo reported his shirt missing and had to ask for another one. Said he was coming from another job and had it in his bag, but when he went to put it on, it was gone."

"That just goes to prove that we were right," Seth said. "Hank stole the shirt and put it on in order to gain access to staff areas."

"Who was the staff person?" Tonya asked.

Clay consulted his notes. "Someone named Brian Lee."

"I know him," Tonya said. "He works a lot of the rodeos."

"We'll track him down and see what he can tell us." He nodded to the door. "I'll follow you back to the ranch. I have a couple of deputies who will be taking turns watching the place. Even have a few off-duty officer buddies from Nashville who've volunteered to spend some time here helping out, too, so we're well covered."

"I can't tell you how much I appreciate it."

Tonya and Seth climbed into Seth's truck and he turned the vehicle toward home. Clay fell in behind them.

They drove in silence for the next few minutes and Tonya figured Seth was doing what she was. Processing. It was a lot to take in. The fact that someone could want her dead simply because she didn't return his affection was beyond crazy. And frankly, if it hadn't been happening to her, she wouldn't have believed it.

"Where's he going?" Seth asked.

"What do you mean? Where's who going?"

"Clay. He just pulled off." He unclipped his cell phone from his belt and passed it to her. "Can you call him and ask him what's going on? He's number three on speed dial."

"Of course." She pressed the button. The phone rang four times, then went to voice mail. She hung up. "He's not answering."

The frown stayed on Seth's face and he pulled into the parking lot of a gas station that had long since closed down. He tapped his fingers on the wheel. "The only reason he'd turn off is if he knew we weren't in any danger."

"And the only way he'd know that is if he knew where Hank was," she said.

Seth nodded. "All right. We'll just keep going. He'll call when he can." Seth pulled back out into the street and headed for the physical therapist's office. Tonya leaned her head back and sent up prayers. Hope dared to sprout.

Seth was right. His brother never would have left them alone if they were still at risk. He knew where Hank was.

The phone rang and she looked at the screen. "It's Clay." She handed the phone to him.

"Where'd you go?" Seth listened, then shot Tonya a victorious smile. "They've got him in custody."

Relief crashed through her. The small seed of hope bloomed into a giddy gladness that made her light-headed. "Really?"

"Really. He's being taken into an interrogation room as we speak." He turned his attention back to the phone. "So you have enough to keep him?" More listening. "Okay, keep us updated." He hung up and parked in front of the physical therapist's office.

Tonya didn't move from her seat. She simply stared out the window. "I want to talk to him."

"What?"

"I have to, Seth."

"No, you don't."

"If I don't, I'll never get past this fear, this hold he has on me. I want to see him." Lifting her chin, she turned to him. "Correction. I don't *want* to—I *have* to."

"And there's nothing I can do to talk you out of this?"

"No."

"Fine." He shoved a hand through his hair and sighed. "We can see what Clay says. I'm guessing they'll hold Newman here in Wrangler's Corner, question him, then move him to Nashville."

"Then take me to see him, please."

It was a small jail. Six cells for simply holding prisoners until they could be transferred to a prison in Nashville. Hank Newman sat in the second cell on the right.

Heart thundering in her throat, Tonya approached it. Seth stayed right next to her and she appreciated his nearness.

His strength and unwavering support.

She stopped in front of the cell and looked at the man who lay on the cot in the corner. Hank Newman. The subject of her nightmares. The reason she'd had limited contact with her family. Seeing him behind bars gave her such a sense of relief she almost couldn't speak. And seeing him also confirmed that he'd been the one who'd followed her into the storage room at the arena. Not that she'd really doubted it, but his appearance was quite different. All except his eyes.

"How did you find me?" She was surprised how steady her voice was. Even with the bars between them, she still wanted to flee. Seth placed a hand on her back and she drew in a deep breath.

Hank simply looked at her. She met him stare for stare, refusing to look away, to give him the satisfaction of seeing her cower before him. She lifted her chin and narrowed her eyes.

A slight smirk curved his lips. He sat up, his dark gaze still locked with hers. "So kind of you to pay me a visit."

She gave a light snort and felt her nerves ease slightly. "Kindness had nothing to do with it. How did you find me?"

He shrugged. "A little birdie told me."

So someone really had told him? "What's kind is for that someone to pay you ten thousand dollars to kill me."

His brows rose. "Hmm."

"Who paid you, Hank?"

He sighed. "No one. I'd been saving for a while and just simply made a deposit before coming to watch the rodeo. Nothing illegal about that."

"It's illegal to break into someone's home and try to

strangle her. It's illegal to shoot at two people riding in the woods. It's illegal—"

He held up a hand and frowned. "What are you talking about? I didn't shoot at you."

She snorted. "Right."

He leaned forward and it was all Tonya could do not to step back. Her pulse still thundered, but she was in control. Hank was once again behind bars and he could no longer hurt her. "You're a liar," she said softly. "A pathetic liar and I almost feel sorry for you." She turned on her heel and nodded to Clay, who twisted the knob.

"I'm not a liar," he called. "I'm many things, but I've never lied to you!" She turned back, almost believing him. He grinned and the lack of...anything, the emptiness in his eyes, chilled her all over again. How had she fallen for his smarmy charm and fakeness? She'd been so blind. He nodded. "You know I'm right. But it doesn't matter. You should have just married me, Tonya. All this could have been avoided if you'd just married me."

She gave him her back without another word. Clay opened the door and she stepped into the hall. Seth reached for her and she slipped into his arms and laid her head against his chest. His heart beat as fast as hers. "Thank you," she murmured.

"For what?"

"Being here."

"Nowhere I'd rather be."

And standing there in his arms, her past finally behind her sitting in a jail cell, she decided she was just fine to let him hold her.

Clay cleared his throat and Seth gently pushed her back from him, glanced at his brother, then back at her. He cupped her chin. "I hate to be the one to say this, but you realize this isn't over, don't you?"

"What do you mean?"

Clay crossed his arms. "My brother's right. Hank may be in jail, but he recently deposited a large sum of money into his bank account. I won't rest easy until I know why."

She frowned. "Like I said before, it just doesn't make any sense. Why would someone pay Hank to kill me? Who knows enough of our relationship to even think of doing it?"

"Well, Hank didn't pay *himself* ten thousand dollars, so this isn't over yet."

By Wednesday morning, Seth was ready to concede that maybe Hank had been working alone. All had been quiet even though Clay hadn't called off the officers watching the house. Contrary to what Seth thought, however, Clay was still convinced Hank hadn't been working alone.

Seth propped his sore leg on the ottoman and leaned back in his father's favorite recliner. Tonya had been gold around the ranch, working and helping like one of the hands. His parents were crazy about her and Seth had to admit he could understand that. She'd been quiet and preoccupied since seeing Hank in the jail but had talked to her family, who'd said they planned to come for the rodeo. "*If* I ride in it," Tonya had told him.

He'd nodded. "That's your call at this point. I thought once Hank was out of the picture..." He'd shrugged. "But if there's someone else involved, I'm inclined to agree it might not be the best idea. But it's been quiet, so..." He'd spread his hands. "I don't know what to tell you."

"I know. I don't know which way to go with this. I'm already committed, so..." She'd sighed and gone back to working on the saddle she'd been cleaning.

His phone rang, pulling him from his thoughts. It was Clay. "Hey there, big brother. What's up?"

"I just got some information I thought I'd pass on to you."

"What's that?"

"Our computer guy was able to enlarge the badge enough to see the name. John Dough. Spelled *D-O-U-G-H.*"

Seth groaned. "Seriously?"

"Yeah. Someone with some skills was able to duplicate one of the badges, print it off and make it look authentic. But there's no way that's a real name."

"Great."

"Yep. Just wanted to let you know."

"Thanks."

Seth hung up, pinched the bridge of his nose, then decided he needed to talk to someone. He dialed his buddy Jake. "'Lo?"

"You sleeping in the middle of the day?"

"Glory was over here last night whining about the rodeo being canceled and wondering what she was going to do in the meantime. Just FYI…she was also full of regrets about walking out on you."

Seth's heart didn't even twinge. He smiled. "That's because Jodie's not in the top fifteen anymore." He held no ill will toward Glory. Instead he just felt sad for her.

"Yeah, that's what I figured."

Jodie McDonald had been one of the favored riders to be headed to the NFR in Las Vegas in December this year. When Seth had been knocked out of last year's finals, Jodie had been bumped up to the fifteenth spot, squeaking his way in. Glory had latched on to him like a leech. Only now Jodie had had two bad rides and was lagging behind at around the seventeenth spot. "Poor Glory." He sighed. "She'll figure it out one day."

"One can hope. And who knows? Maybe Jodie will have a miraculous comeback? Kinda like someone else we know?" He cleared his throat. "So how are you doing? You at your parents' ranch?"

Seth sat up and put his feet on the floor. He ignored the twinge in his leg. At least it was feeling better. He'd been doing his physical therapy exercises even though he'd skipped the appointment on Monday. He'd been a bit preoccupied. "I am."

"Man, it's been crazy around here. Wish I had some place to escape to."

"You're still at the arena?"

"They're letting us stay put for now. Looks like the rodeo might happen week after next."

"Cool. I'll put it on my calendar." He'd been so out of touch he hadn't heard that the event had been rescheduled.

"You riding in the Wrangler's Corner rodeo that's starting this Thursday?"

"Yep. I'm all signed up."

"Think I might join you."

Seth frowned. "Why would you do that?"

"Got nothing better to do and it would be fun to raise money for charity. You got that little RV park on the outskirts of town, right?"

"Yeah, but—"

"No buts. I'm tired of this sitting around. I'm coming."

"Well…all right, then." There was no stopping Jake once he got his mind set on something and Seth wouldn't even try. "Hey, I've got an idea. We'll add Daniel's Li'l Buckaroo charity to the list and win some money for it. What do you say?"

Jake stayed silent for a long second, then cleared his throat. "I think that would be an excellent thing to do.

Daniel would be thrilled we'd do it. I'll tell Monty. I know he'll want to come, too."

"That sounds like a good plan."

"Hey, you heard from Tonya?"

"I—" Seth paused. He didn't want to lie, but he wasn't about to tell Jake that she was at the ranch and have his buddy mention that to the wrong person. "I think Tonya's lying low right now until it's all worked out with the guy that was after her." No sense in saying anything about Hank being in jail. Seth had a feeling that didn't matter, that someone else was interested in getting Tonya out of the picture. Jake didn't need to know that either.

"All right," Jake said. "Y'all need help setting up?"

"Aaron's part of the crew that's in charge. He's already storing stuff in the barn. We might need your truck to haul some of it to the arena when the time comes."

"You got it."

"Hey, while I'm thinking about it, will you get my rope from the storage room? Mia said she hung it there. I want to take a look at it."

"Sure thing."

Seth hung up with Jake and pursed his lips. It would be good to have everyone together at the rodeo, but it also made him nervous. "Hank's behind bars. It'll be all right." But whoever had paid him ten grand wasn't—

"Talking to yourself?"

Seth looked up to find his brother Aaron in the doorway. "I always ask advice from the wisest person I know." Aaron rolled his blue eyes and smirked. Seth could have been looking into a mirror. All the Starke brothers resembled one another, but Seth and Aaron could have been twins if they hadn't been born two years apart.

"How's the leg?" Aaron asked.

"Fine." He was so tired of everyone asking about it

but knew they just asked out of concern, so he hid his annoyance and ordered himself to be grateful they cared. "What brings you by?"

Aaron jerked a thumb toward the barn. "I've got one last truckload of rodeo stuff to unload."

"You need help?" Seth started to stand.

Aaron shook his head. "I brought my help. Just wanted to let someone know we were here. Where are Mom and Dad?"

Seth sank back onto the chair. "Think they're doing their weekly grocery run."

"All right. Dad said he had a horse he wanted me to take a look at."

"Probably Thunder."

Aaron nodded. "I'll be in the barn."

Seth stood. "I might as well come along."

Seth followed his brother out to the front porch. He descended the steps and headed down the path that would lead to the barn. "How's the veterinary business going?"

"Staying busy, that's for sure. Meeting some interesting people."

Seth slid a glance at Aaron. "Anyone in particular?"

"Nope."

"Liar." Aaron flushed and laughed. They reached the barn and Seth could tell his brother wasn't going to tell him whom he was talking about. "I'll find out, you know."

"Yeah. Probably." He waved to the two men sitting on the edge of the back of the loaded pickup truck. "Seth, you remember Randy? And this is Bill. You guys ready?"

"Just waiting on you," Randy said.

"All right, let's get all this stuff stored in the back of the barn. There's a huge empty area just around the corner from the office."

The three men got busy and Seth decided to pitch in and do what he could.

It didn't take long for the four of them to get everything loaded and in place with room for more if needed. Seth was grateful his leg didn't bother him more than a few twinges if he moved wrong. "You know, it would be nice if we could just have some sort of storage pod over near the arena. This event gets bigger every year. Pretty soon the barn isn't going to be big enough."

Aaron shoved a barrel against the wall and turned to face him. "Yep. I suggested that very thing for next year. Hauling all this stuff to two places is downright ridiculous." When the rodeo had been just a local event, it hadn't been any big deal. Participants had just brought their stuff with them when they got there. Now the bigger names were shipping their gear and it was getting hectic. "This is the last year we're doing it this way."

"Seth?"

He spun to find Tonya watching the proceedings. She looked beautiful. And contemplative. "You have impeccable timing," he said, wiping the sweat from his forehead. "We just finished."

She laughed, but it didn't hold much humor or reach her eyes.

"What's wrong?"

"Nothing, just a feeling I can't shake."

Seth walked over and placed his hands on her shoulders. "Everything's going to work out fine. You'll see."

"You're the eternal optimist, aren't you?"

He tilted his head. "Hmm. Only around you. I think you bring that out in me."

She gave him a small smile. "I came out here to tell you that I'm having second thoughts about tomorrow."

"Bullfighting?"

"Yes. What if whoever paid Hank uses tomorrow as an opportunity to finish the job?"

"How would he know you're there?"

Tonya propped her hands on her hips. "You signed me up, remember?"

"I sure did." He winked. "But I didn't use your real name."

Her eyes widened. "Really? Who am I, then?"

"Betty Benson."

The laughter escaped her and his heart twisted around itself at the sound. Seth finally had to admit that in spite of all of his mental barriers and adamant protesting, he was falling hard for the rodeo clown. He just wondered how she would react when he told her.

SIXTEEN

Tonya lay in bed, nervous about the show the next day. *God, I just don't know if I should do this. I know Hank's behind bars, but—*

She gave a low groan, sat up and threw the covers off. Then she walked to the motor-home window and pushed the drapes aside. A cruiser sat parked in plain sight of anyone driving up the drive. Tonya knew another was behind the house with a good view of the trees and pastureland, should someone decide to approach from that angle. She offered a prayer of safety for each officer and asked God to bless them for their willingness to watch over her while missing out on time with their families.

A faint light caught her attention and she squinted, trying to see through the darkness. The light bounced a couple of times, then disappeared. Should she worry about it? Go investigate? Not by herself, for sure, but she wondered if Seth was still up. His trailer was parked just a few steps from hers. She snagged her cell phone and dialed his number.

It went to voice mail, so she tried again.

"Hello?" He sounded groggy, as if she'd woken him up.

"Seth, I saw a light out by the barn."

"What? When?"

"Just a minute ago." Not too much time had passed. "Should we alert the deputies?"

He paused. "Maybe. What kind of light?"

"I don't know. Just a light." She thought of the brief bobbing motion. "Maybe like someone carrying a flashlight."

"Well, it wouldn't be one of the hands. They've all gone home." She heard rustling in the background. "I'll take care of it. You stay put."

"But—"

"I'll get Ronnie to go with me."

That mollified her. Ronnie was in the cruiser nearest the house. "All right. Be careful. Please?"

"Of course."

She hung up and peeked out the window toward the barn again. Nothing. Had she imagined the light? No. She knew she'd seen it. Seth appeared in a T-shirt and jeans and his ever-present boots. He came down the steps of his fifth wheel and headed toward Ronnie's cruiser.

Tonya slipped out the door and sat on the top step. She heard their voices but couldn't catch the words. Rising to her feet, she moved closer, staying in the shadows up close to the side of the motor home. Not wanting to interfere but not willing to sit inside and twiddle her thumbs either. If someone else was involved in this campaign to kill her, she wanted to know who it was.

She tightened her jaw and drew in a deep breath. Seth and Ronnie headed for the barn with Ronnie speaking into his radio. Another officer joined them. The three men disappeared into the nearest door. All remained quiet. She could hear her heart beating a triple-time rhythm. She placed a hand over her chest and waited.

The barn door creaked when Seth shut it behind him. He stuffed the key in his pocket and tried to figure out how someone could be inside when the barn was kept locked up. The two officers moved in front of him, Ronnie's admonitions about staying outside or going back to his fifth wheel falling on deaf ears. No way. This was his family's property. If someone was here determined to cause mischief or do Tonya harm, Seth was equally determined to stop them.

Ronnie dimmed the flashlight beam to almost nothing. Seth reached for the light switch and felt Lance's hand clamp down on his forearm. "If you flip the lights we're instant targets."

"Right."

"Stay here. Don't move. I'm serious," Lance ordered.

"Got it."

He dropped his hand and listened. Nothing sounded out of place; nothing *felt* different. The two officers began their search with Seth standing just inside the door. He knew why they didn't want him to move. If something happened and they had to use their weapons, they didn't want him caught in the cross fire. He didn't want that either. What he wanted was to know what light Tonya thought she'd seen. The night-lights in the barn were doing their job and he could see shadows, but up against the wall, he knew he would be practically invisible to anyone looking in his direction.

The horses nickered and blew and stomped at the disruption of their nightly routine. Ronnie and Lance disappeared from view as they searched the barn, turning left at the corner of the L-shaped building. Seth hesitated, almost followed them, then slipped back out of the barn. He made his way across the packed dirt and went straight for Tonya's motor home.

He gave a soft rap on her door, then glanced back over his shoulder.

"Seth?"

He whirled to find Tonya standing behind him. "What are you doing out here?"

"Figured I could see and hear better out here than in there."

He shook his head. "That's not smart."

"I know."

Her subdued tone worried him. "Let's get inside."

"Did they find anything?"

"Not at the time I left. They asked me to stay put, but I got to thinking about it and didn't want you left alone."

They moved inside the motor home and she flipped on a small lamp. It was cool and cozy in the vehicle. He sat in the recliner next to the door. She took the couch opposite. "So we wait?"

"We wait. But I also wanted to tell you that we're going to have visitors tomorrow."

"Visitors?"

"I talked to Jake earlier and he's decided he wants to ride in the rodeo this weekend. Since the cutoff date to register is right up to the last minute, it's not an issue. He and Monty and some of the barrel racers are going to be here tomorrow morning. Some may have even arrived this evening."

Her eyes went wide. "That's great. I'm so glad."

He nodded, stood and went to the window to push the curtain aside. Still no movement from the barn. What was taking so long? Had they found something? He glanced at the main house. No lights were on; no one seemed to be disturbed by anything.

He drew in a deep breath and turned back to find Tonya in the small kitchen making a pot of coffee. "I hope that's decaf."

She glanced at him. "Yep."

"I'll take some when it's ready, then."

She nodded and pressed the button to start brewing. "The lights are on in the barn."

He took a look. "Maybe they found something."

"Should we go out there?"

"No. Let's just wait."

She shifted, tapped her foot, paced to the window then back to the kitchen area. She finally sighed and pulled two mugs from the cabinet.

Seth hated that he couldn't do anything about the worry and the tense set of her posture. He walked up behind her, settling his hands on her shoulders. "It's going to be all right."

"So you keep saying."

His fingers massaged her, moving in tight circles against the rigid muscles. She didn't pull away and didn't tell him to stop, so he kept it up. She let her head fall back against his chest and closed her eyes. He kept working the muscles, feeling them loosen a fraction, then a bit more. His heart tumbled from caution straight into love. A tremor ran through him and he turned her to face him. She opened her sky blue eyes and he knew he was lost. He might as well give in, because to fight it was a losing battle. "Tonya—"

Her eyes widened; her cheeks grew flushed. She shook her head. "Not yet, Seth," she whispered. "Don't say anything yet." Frustration ran through him. But she was right: now wasn't the time. He was beginning to wonder if the right time would ever come.

A knock on the door made them both jump, but Seth beat her to the window. He pushed aside the curtain and looked out. Lance stood at the bottom of the steps. Seth opened the door. "You find anything?"

The deputy shook his head. "We didn't find a person,

but do you recognize this?" In a gloved hand, he held up a silver pen with a brown-and-red logo on the side.

Seth moved closer to get a better look. "It's from the rodeo that was canceled last weekend. They have them at all the tables to sign up for prizes and stuff." He glanced at Tonya. "Did you possibly drop that in the barn when you were helping?"

"No, I didn't even pick one up. Too busy."

"I didn't either." Seth leaned back. "So someone who was at the rodeo last weekend was in the barn and dropped the pen. *Tonight*." He looked at Lance. "Where did you find it?"

"Near the last stall on the right, just before the storage area you've got back there. I turned the lights on to take one last sweep through the place and found this."

Tonya rubbed her forehead. "Great. Why would someone from last week's rodeo be in your barn?"

Seth flattened his lips. "Could be someone looking for something he or she shipped here and didn't want to wake us up to ask for it." He shrugged. "It's common knowledge where their items are stored. Wouldn't be the first time someone's come looking for something."

She lifted a brow. "In the middle of the night?"

"Okay, yes. This is a first."

"So what does it mean?"

He grimaced. "Just means someone who was at the rodeo last week was in the barn. At one o'clock in the morning the night before the rodeo."

"You don't keep the barn locked up?" Lance asked.

"Of course. You saw me unlock it in order to let you guys in." He kneaded the back of his neck.

Lance nodded. "All right, well, it's all clear out there for now. We didn't hear any engines start up or anyone running away. We canvassed the trees on the other side of the barn, as well, but there's a lot of land out there. If someone was in the barn, it wouldn't be hard to find a good hiding spot."

"Don't I know it," Seth muttered.

At Tonya's raised brow, he shrugged. "Childhood memories."

"So what now?" she asked.

"Go back to sleep. We'll keep an eye on everything, mostly where you two are, and make sure nothing else happens tonight."

"How did you miss someone going into the barn?" Seth asked with a frown. Lance sighed. "It really wouldn't be hard. Even if we knew someone was coming and also the direction he was coming from, we still might overlook him if he was dressed in black and being careful to avoid any sudden movements."

"We'll leave the lights on in the barn and the perimeter lights. That'll make that area fairly glow. Nothing I can do about the back of the main house without waking my parents." Seth glanced at the house. "Can't believe they've slept through this."

Tonya agreed. But the officers had been quiet and nothing had happened that would wake anyone sleeping. "Thank you again for everything," she said softly.

Lance nodded. "Oh, by the way, Ronnie and I are transferring Hank to the Nashville prison tomorrow. We thought we were going to have to let him go, but his prints came back on the bomb that was in your cannon, so he's going away for a while. Get some rest—you're going to need it tomorrow."

The deputy left and Tonya dropped onto the couch. "Tomorrow." She glanced at the clock. "Which is actually today."

"All right, if you're good here, I'm going to head back to my place."

"I'm good. I'm very good. Hank's not getting out of jail for a long time."

"But there's still someone else out there who wants to hurt you." He moved close and crouched down in front of her. "You want to move into the main house for the rest of the night?"

"No. I trust Lance and Ronnie. They won't let anything happen. And besides, it would wake up your parents. I'll be fine." She stared into his deep blue eyes and did her best to ignore the intense feelings his nearness brought to the surface. After their tender moment earlier, she wondered if she should even fight them.

Remember Daniel.

He gripped her hands and kissed her on the cheek. "Good night, then, Tonya."

She swallowed hard and felt tears surface. She managed to hold them back and give him a nod. He left and she wanted to call him back. Tonya sighed and locked the door after him. Her heart was turning traitor. Her mind ordered it to do one thing and it did the complete opposite. She looked out the window one more time and took comfort in the fact that the officers were there and watching tonight.

But she couldn't help wondering what tomorrow would bring. A Bible verse from Philippians popped into her mind. *Do not be anxious about anything, but in every situation, by prayer and petition, with thanksgiving, present your requests to God.*

"God," she whispered, "I'm going to try not to be anxious, but it sure is hard. Thank You for Seth and his family and the men sitting in the cruisers outside. Please, please let them catch whoever is causing all this trouble and keep everyone safe tomorrow." Tonya left the lights on and moved to the back of the motor home to the bed. She lay down, still fully dressed, and pulled the covers to her chin as she debated how to tell Seth she wasn't going to the rodeo in the morning.

A sudden resolve sat her straight up. Scratch that. She *wasn't* going to run away again. This time Tonya was going to stand her ground. She was going to the rodeo and she was going to figure out who the other person was who wanted her dead.

Or she would die trying.

SEVENTEEN

Thursday morning found the sun breaking through the clouds as though eager to get the day started. Tonya couldn't say she felt the same, but her middle-of-the-night resolve hadn't wavered. She was still determined to do this. But the knowledge that her family was going to be there terrified her. She called Grant and told him not to come.

"Too late. And if you're still in danger, this time we're all fighting back."

Uncertainty tried to wrangle its way in and she shoved it aside. Security was tight enough for a presidential visit thanks to Clay and his Nashville resources. It would be all right. She almost smiled at the thought. Seth's optimism was starting to rub off on her.

She and Seth arrived at the arena early. Staff was working hard, setting up and getting ready for the first event, which would start at six o'clock that evening. Some vendors had already shown up and gotten started on the setup, parking their motor homes and RVs and fifth wheels in the large lot behind the arena.

Tonya stepped from the truck and ran her already sweaty palms down the front of her jeans. She could do this. She *would* do this. Her eyes searched the growing crowd and fell on a familiar face just as the woman bent to fill her cup with water from the jug. "Mia!"

Her friend paused for a brief moment, then turned from the water station, her eyes wide. "Tonya? I thought that was your voice! What are you doing here?" She set her cup on the table and closed the distance to grab Tonya in a bone-crushing hug. "Are you all right? Where've you been? I want to hear everything. Tell me!"

Tonya gave a breathless laugh and extracted herself from her best friend's grip. The tall dark-haired beauty looked tired and stressed, but Tonya was so glad to see her. "I'm fine. I'm okay. At least for now. How are you? You been sleeping okay?"

Mia waved a hand. "It's been a stressful few days. But forget about that. What about that guy that was stalking you? Hank?"

"They caught him. He's in jail. I think he's supposed to be transferred to Nashville sometime today."

"Oh, wow. That's crazy. I'm so glad you're okay." Mia gave her a quick hug. "Still, you'd better watch your back."

"What do you mean?"

Mia grimaced. "Glory's here."

Tonya nearly wilted in relief. "Oh. Okay. Thanks for the heads-up." The last person she was worried about was Seth's ex-girlfriend. She didn't necessarily want to go to lunch with the woman, but she could be civil if she happened to run into her.

"Well, I gotta go," Mia said, glancing at her watch. "I've got to walk the dogs and make sure I'm ready for tonight. They're letting me do an abbreviated version of one of my shows."

"You'll be great. I'll see you later."

Mia rushed off in the direction of the motor-home

parking and Tonya turned to see Seth in deep conversation with Clay. Her heart thudded that extra beat as it always did when he was around. He looked amazing in his rodeo attire. Chaps covered his jeans, and his plaid shirt was tucked in, showing off his trim waist. His hat sat cocked at an angle, revealing his strong features. Features that looked strained. She moved toward the men. "What's going on?"

Seth held up a rope. "Jake brought this to me. It's the one I used the day I fell last week. Mia said she hung it in the storage area for me to pick up when I could, but Jake said it wasn't there when he went to get it. He said he looked around but finally had to give up and get on the road. At the last minute, he decided to clean the trash out of his truck—" At Tonya's raised brow, he nodded. "Yes, he was really going to do that. Anyway, he drove around to the Dumpster and found this lying on the ground next to it."

"Someone tried to throw it away?"

"Someone in a hurry. They missed."

"But why?"

He grabbed two pieces and held them out to her. "To get rid of the evidence. See anything wrong with this?"

She gasped. "Part of it's been cut."

Seth's heart still pounded in his chest as his gaze swung between his brother and Tonya. Her face had gone white and Clay looked ready to use his weapon on the person who'd cut the rope. Assuming he could find him. The rope had been sliced almost in half. The bucking and rocking of the bull and Seth's tight grip had been enough to break it the rest of the way.

Tonya stared at him, her blue eyes shimmering with fear. "Who could have done such a thing? You put that rope on yourself."

"I don't know. It's crazy sometimes when I'm getting ready to get on the bull. People hanging over the fence, holding the rope so I can tie my hand." He shrugged. "I can't remember all the people there. Jake and Monty and—" He blew out a sigh. "I just don't know. I wasn't paying attention. I was trying to keep my focus on the ride." And his stomach from losing what little he'd eaten that day.

"So why would someone want to sabotage your ride?" she asked. It was a rhetorical question. She knew the answer as well as he did; he could see the knowledge in her eyes.

His jaw tightened and he answered it anyway. "Because I'm winning a lot of money and I'm going to the NFR in December. If I get injured and can't go, someone else gets to take my place."

"But who? I can't believe it. *Who?*"

Clay stepped forward. "Who stands to gain the most if you don't ride in the finals, Seth?"

"Whoever would slide in my spot should I fall off the list."

"That would be Jodie," Tonya said.

Seth shook his head. "Actually, I think it's Monty. Jodie's at number seventeen. Monty's at number sixteen."

Clay nodded. "I'll find him. And if you insist on riding today, you better make sure you've got a good rope on there and people you trust around the pen."

"I'll be on the alert."

"I've got a prisoner to get ready for transport, but I'll be back later this afternoon," Clay said.

Seth nodded and his brother headed to his cruiser, climbed in and drove away.

Tonya stared at him. "Are you still going to ride?"

Seth narrowed his eyes. "Not only that, but I'm going

to win." At her blink, he softened his stance. "I know this ride isn't going to be about the money or the finals. It's about the principle of the thing."

"I understand." She placed a hand on his arm. "Seth, someone was in the barn last night," she reminded him. "Could that person have been looking for some of your gear to try and sabotage you again?"

Seth froze. She was right. "My initials are all over my gear," he said. "It wouldn't take much to figure out what belonged to me. But someone dropped the pen near the storage room, not the tack room, where I keep my gear."

She shrugged. "I don't know, but you need to be real careful."

He nodded and frowned. "We both do."

"Tonya? Honey?"

Tonya whirled at the familiar voice. She hesitated less than a second before she hurled herself into the familiar arms. "Mom." Tears leaked, then streamed. She pulled back and looked the woman full in the face. "You haven't changed a bit."

"Oh, sweetheart, you're such a liar. Missing you has aged me considerably."

"Well, maybe it's because I can't see through my tears very well, but you look exactly the same to me."

Her mother pulled her back into a hug and just held her while they both cried.

"Hey, Clown. Enough of that crying stuff. I need a hug, too."

Tonya looked up to find her brother Grant and her father, Doug, standing off to the side scuffing their feet and peering at her from the corners of their eyes. She hugged one, then the other, relishing the reality of their presence. Finally, she sniffed and scrubbed at her face with the only thing she had available: her shirtsleeve.

Her mother stuffed tissues into her hand. "I came prepared."

Tonya gave a shaky laugh. "Thanks." She mopped up her face as best she could. And remembered Seth. She turned to find him watching the whole thing with a smile on his handsome face. And was that a tear in his eye? She held out a hand and he stepped forward. "Seth, this is part of my family. Mom, Dad, Grant, this is Seth. I've been staying with his family. If you've talked to Clay, that's his brother."

Tonya's mom moved forward to hug Seth. "Thank you for keeping her safe."

Seth flushed and hugged her back. "It was my pleasure, ma'am. I've grown pretty fond of...uh... Clown?"

Tonya turned a glare on Grant, who feigned a duck. "Don't let her hurt me."

Tonya shook her head and scowled. "You're the one who should have the nickname Clown."

Tonya's father stepped forward for another hug. "We know you're busy, baby, but we couldn't wait to see you. I talked to Deputy Starke this morning and he said Hank was going behind bars for a long time."

Tonya bit her lip and nodded as reality intruded. "Yes. Yes, he is. I'll have to testify again, but he won't be getting off as easy. He planted a bomb that could have hurt a lot of people. Apparently that's more serious than trying to strangle someone, but that's all right—I'll take it."

Tonya's mother held her arms out for another hug. "We drove the motor home, so we'll be there resting while you get ready for tonight. We'll see you soon, okay?"

"Perfect. I'm so glad to see you all."

"Us too, honey, us too."

Her family walked away and it was all she could do

not to bolt after them, touch them, hug them, talk to them. Just to make sure they were really there.

"Come on, *Clown*. We have a rodeo to get ready for," Seth said.

"And equipment to go over with a fine-tooth comb."

"Ma'am?"

Tonya turned to find a large man in a Tennessee police uniform standing behind her. "Yes?"

"Are you Tonya Waters?"

"I am."

He held out a hand. "I'm Officer Richard Abbott. Clay asked me to make sure you have security with you at all times."

"A bodyguard?" she asked.

"Something like that." His smile revealed even white teeth in his tanned face. "Clay explained what was going on with you. I'm going to hang near but won't interfere with anything you need."

Her gaze bounced between the officer and Seth. "I'm really not sure I'm the one who needs the bodyguard anymore. I think Seth is the one who might need the extra protection."

Seth shook his head, crossing his arms stubbornly over his chest. "I'm fine. I'm going to check out my gear and make sure it's good to go. And then I'm going to recheck it minutes before I'm supposed to ride. He stays with you."

She hesitated, still unsure, then nodded. He would be smart. And so would she. "All right, Officer Abbott, let's go find the dressing room."

EIGHTEEN

The work progressed pretty quickly. Seth ended up helping Aaron distribute the gear to those who'd shipped it or dropped it off. He had help, but it was never enough and no one was about to turn away his extra pair of hands. Time passed and he finally caught sight of Monty. Anger bubbled beneath the surface at the thought that the man could do something so underhanded. Then again, he didn't have proof that his buddy had actually done it. Seth would hold his tongue until something was proved.

Before he knew it, the afternoon was gone and he was starving. He hadn't seen much of Tonya since she'd left with the security guard, but every once in a while she would wave at him while on her way to do whatever task she had to get done. Her police-officer bodyguard trailed faithfully behind, staying close enough to ease Seth's mind. And every time he saw someone from the rodeo last weekend, he couldn't help but wonder if he or she was the one who'd dropped the pen in the barn.

"Hey."

Seth looked up to find Tonya standing next to him and the empty truck bed. "Hey yourself."

She held out an aluminum-wrapped burger. He snagged it. "Aaron's gone to get us some food, but this will make a nice appetizer. Bless you." He opened the burger and took a huge bite.

"Guess I should have gotten three or four."

"Nah, I'll have to wait to eat a real meal until after I ride. Don't want to embarrass myself out there." He took a closer look at her pale face. His hunger faded. "What's wrong?"

"Clay just called. He tried you first but couldn't get you."

Seth patted his belt where he usually carried his phone. He'd stuck it on the front seat of Aaron's truck so he wouldn't catch it on anything. "What is it?"

"Hank escaped."

Tonya heard the words leave her lips but almost couldn't process what she was saying. Seth's jaw went tight and his eyes narrowed. "What? How?"

"He had help. They were on their way to the Nashville prison. Clay said Ronnie and Lance had him in the car when, about ten minutes outside Nashville, Hank started vomiting. They pulled over and got him out of the car. Someone started shooting at them and Ronnie was hit. He's in the hospital, but he's alive and will be all right. Lance fired back, but Hank managed to crawl away while whoever was helping him kept Lance from doing anything."

"They didn't have him cuffed?" Seth's shock echoed through the barn. The other men had stopped and were listening.

"Yes, of course, but that didn't stop him from slithering away like the snake he is. He even managed to get Lance's gun on his way to freedom." Seth heard the bitterness in her voice and didn't blame her. She shook her head. "I should have known," she whispered. "We've thought all along he was working with someone. Now we know for sure."

Seth ran a weary hand over his brow. "And now he has a gun."

"Yes."

"And he's on the loose again."

"Yes. Which means he's probably heading this way."

Seth glanced at his watch. "The rodeo starts in thirty minutes. Clay will have notified security here. You've got Officer Abbott here on you. I've checked my gear and all is fine." He took a deep breath. "I think we'll be all right. Everyone will be on the lookout for Hank. He'll lie low for a while."

Tonya pursed her lips and studied him. He could see her thinking. She finally gave a slow nod. "All right. You could be right. Let's not let the possibility of him showing up ruin this. Let's trust security to do their jobs so we can do ours."

"Deal." He hugged her tight and placed a kiss on the top of her head. *God, please don't let anything happen to her.* "Now, let's go win some money for some Li'l Buckaroos."

Tonya nodded. "Yeah. Let's do that."

"We're one of the first events, so we're going to have to hurry." Seth looked up to find Aaron coming toward him. "Hang on to that food. I'm going to need it before too long."

His brother nodded and tossed the food bags into the front seat of his truck. "Don't fall off this time. It's only eight seconds."

"I appreciate the concern and the support."

Aaron turned serious. "I mean it."

"I know you do."

Aaron man-hugged him and moved away. Seth gave

him a two-fingered salute and followed Tonya to the arena and around to the dressing room. "See you soon."

"Yeah. Be careful, Seth."

"Always."

He locked his gaze on hers and swooped in for a swift kiss. "We're going to talk."

"I know."

"Okay, then." He turned away and caught Officer Abbott's gaze. He nodded. The officer nodded back. Good— they understood each other.

Seth entered the men's dressing room and waded through the participants, accepting slaps on the back and *welcome home*s with a smile and words of thanks. But his mind was on Tonya, Hank's escape and the long eight seconds coming up.

Tonya rolled the barrel into the arena one more time. Monty had ridden first, then Jake. Now Seth was up. Mia had done her quick show with the dogs and the audience was still cheering for her. Now it was Tonya's turn to bullfight for Seth. Mia would join her in seconds as soon as she had the dogs put up.

Her heart fluttered in her chest. Tonya knew she had to get her mind in the game and off the fear that Hank would show up instead of deciding to lie low. She glanced at the barrel and thought it felt a bit lighter than usual but didn't think anything about it as her gaze sought Seth. There he was. Already in the bull pen, getting ready to lower himself on the snorting, pawing beast. She closed her eyes and breathed a quick prayer for his safety. *Please, don't let him fall off.*

She left her barrel in the middle of the ring and moved close to the pen where she would wait for the two other cowboys to pull open the gate. Mia raced out to join her on the opposite side. She watched Seth wrap his hand and test the rope. One pull, two. He looked up and met her gaze. He gave her a quick nod and she answered with the same. He was ready.

And so was she. She glanced at Mia, who nodded.

Tonya scratched her head under the wig and drew in a deep breath. Seth gave the signal he was ready. The crowd stayed silent. The gates opened and the bull shot out, bucking.

Seth held on. Tonya stayed out of the way but close by in case she had to act. Mia did the same, circling the bull, dodging the hooves. Tonya prayed while her adrenaline hummed. The bull spun, flinging Seth sideways, and still he held on, his gloved right hand gripping the rope, his left waving in the air. The time ticked down.

The crowd rose to its feet.

Three…two…one.

The buzzer sounded. The bull kept going, but she could see Seth had his hand free and was ready to jump. Mia backed away as the bull shot his legs into the air. When he touched down again, Seth leaped clear. The crowd roared their cheers.

Tonya sprang into action. Seth was still a good ways from the fence. The animal snorted and bucked his displeasure. His hooves crashed into the dirt and the air seemed to vibrate as he had his full attention on Seth.

Mia grabbed the red cloth and waved it at the bull. The two cowboys who'd opened the gate raced to Seth, who'd already rolled to his feet. The bull charged at them. Mia raced in front of him, flinging the cloth in his face. He stopped in his tracks for a brief second, then shook his head and came after her.

Tonya yelled and raced for the fence. Seth was safe, as was Mia, who'd made it to the other side. But the bull wasn't heading back to the pen as he was supposed to. He whirled and came after her. Tonya knew she'd never make it and bolted for the barrel. She threw herself inside.

And froze.

There were no handles. No aluminum frame. Just wood. Nothing that could stop the bull's horns should he decide to ram one of them. It would go straight through the wood and into her. Someone had switched the barrels. She was dead if she stayed inside, because no one on the outside would know that she wasn't protected. She popped up, terror racing through her. The bull circled her, ducked his head and pawed the ground.

Think, Tonya, think!

The bull charged. Tonya ducked and braced herself. The animal rammed his head against the barrel. Tonya slammed against the side, felt her world tilt, then roll. She heard the crowd's yell, their claps and more cheers. She had to get out.

Or she would be seriously hurt—or dead—within the next few seconds.

NINETEEN

Seth sat on top of the rail and watched the bull ram the barrel. When the sphere came to a stop, his gut tightened as the bull prepared to strike again. He clenched his fist against his left thigh and absently noted that his leg ached but not too bad. And while he noticed that, he had his attention centered on Tonya.

As long as she stayed put, she'd be all right. The other two cowboys were already racing to help, to distract the bull, but he was on his way for another hit.

And Tonya crawled from the barrel.

Seth's heart nearly stopped. He stood on the rail. "What are you doing?" he hissed even though there was no way she'd hear him.

Tonya got to her feet and faced the oncoming bull.

The crowd fell silent as though someone had flipped the switch. This wasn't the way things were supposed to play out and they knew it. She was supposed to wait for one of the others to distract the bull.

Jake stood beside him. "What's she doing? She's going to get herself killed!"

"I don't know. I don't know." Without thinking, he leaped into the arena and hollered for the bull.

Tonya registered Seth's entrance into the arena and the

bull's focus turning. The animal skidded to a stop and all she could think was that history was going to repeat itself. *Not again.* She wouldn't live through another Daniel.

And she couldn't leave Seth to face down the bull alone. He didn't know the tricks of the trade. He was going to die because of her. Because he cared too much. Just like Daniel. Tonya heard Mia's shouts and looked over her shoulder to see her friend waving and calling to her.

But the big animal heard Mia, too, and whirled to come after Tonya one more time. She backed up and, for one brief second, caught Seth's eye. *He's mine. I can do this.*

Seth hollered again. And once again the bull was distracted for a brief moment. She clapped her hands and stomped her feet. Now it was just a show. A competition. And one she planned on winning.

The bull charged her. Closer, closer. The crowd's roars rose once again, then faded to the back of her mind. It was just her and the bull. He thundered nearer. Still she waited.

At just the right moment, she spun.

Right where she wanted to be. In his "pocket," up against the end of his body near his ribs. She faced his tail and waited for him to do the spinning move. He swung his head around and tried to hook her with that deadly horn, but she stayed with him, stepping in tight circles, keeping herself right in his pocket. There was no way he could reach her this way. And the more he spun, the closer she was able to move toward the fence.

She waited, continuing her movements, biding her time. She knew the window of time would be minuscule for her exit. More stepping, more spinning.

And there it was.

She shot straight out, parallel with his hindquarters, faking one way, then throwing herself in the opposite direction. She hit the fence and flipped over.

Safe. Alive. And in Seth's arms.

The crowd went crazy, their roars and applause nothing compared to the admiration and love—and terror—staring down at her.

Seth's heart pounded like a runaway train. She'd done it. She was safe. And she was wrapped up next to him. Right where he'd keep her and never let her go out of his sight again.

She moved against him. And he had no choice but to release his grip. "You're all right."

"I'm fine."

"You scared me."

"You scared *me*. We're even." She looked toward the arena and he let his gaze follow hers. "They got him back in his pen," she said. "Man, what was wrong with him? He was one angry bull."

Before he had a chance to respond, they were swarmed. Back slaps and congrats followed, and Seth gritted his teeth and waited for the hoopla to pass. He wanted to talk to Tonya alone. Finally, the crowd dispersed and Officer Abbott moved in. "Come on. Let's go somewhere a little more private so y'all can catch your breath."

Seth gladly draped an arm around Tonya's shoulders and let Abbott lead the way. He cleared the path, and within a short time they found themselves in the break room. Fortunately, they were the only ones there.

Seth turned her to face him. "I thought he was going to stomp you. What made you get out of your barrel like that? You're not stupid, Tonya, and you're not a grandstander looking for attention, but I can't come up with what would make you do that." He heard the low pulse of anger in his voice, but she'd terrified him.

"It wasn't my barrel."

"What?"

"Someone switched it. I need someone to get it so I can look at it more. I mean, it looks like mine on the outside, but on the inside, it's definitely not mine. It's all wood."

His heart thudded again. "So that's why."

"Yeah."

"You could have been killed."

"I think that was the goal."

He looked at the officer. "May I borrow your phone? I left mine in the locker while I rode."

"Of course." Officer Abbott pulled his from the clip on his already overloaded belt and handed the device to Seth.

He punched in Clay's number. The phone rang, and just when he thought it might go to voice mail, his brother answered. "Clay?"

"Yeah?"

"Get the barrel Tonya left in the ring."

"They've moved it."

"I need you to find it. Someone swapped it out. That's why she got out of it. If she'd stayed in it, she might have been killed."

"What?"

"Just find that barrel."

"Copy that."

He hung up and handed the phone back to the officer. He looked at Tonya's pinched face and settled his hands on her shoulders. "Did you have your barrel stored in the barn?"

"No, it was on my motor home. I just unloaded it and put it with the rest of the gear when we got here."

His mouth tightened. "Maybe the person thought it

was in the barn and went looking for it, didn't find it but got to it here."

"Maybe, but then that means the person has clearance, has access to be in that area."

"That's a lot of people if you count participants, staff and volunteers."

Tonya shook her head. "And I'm guessing this place doesn't have a lot of security cameras."

"There are some, but I don't know where they are."

The officer's phone rang and he unclipped it. Glanced down at the screen and handed it to Seth. "I think it's for you."

Seth took it. "You find the barrel?"

"Yes, we've got it. I've also got some interesting video footage of your ride last weekend. Want to come take a look?"

"Absolutely."

"I'm in the cruiser."

"I'm on the way." He hung up and handed over the phone once again. "I'm going to meet Clay at his car. He wants to show me some video of my fall from last week. You want to come?"

She hesitated. "I think I'm going to wash up and go spend some time with my family while I can."

Seth glanced at the officer and nodded. "All right. I'm good with that. I'll get my phone from the locker first thing. Do you have yours?"

"It's in the women's dressing room. I'll get Officer Abbott to escort me over there so I'll have it."

He leaned over and kissed her. "We're going to get to the bottom of this."

She gave him a tremulous smile. "What happened to 'It's going to be all right'?"

"That too." He looked up at the quiet policeman. "The

guy that's been stalking her escaped. He could show up any moment. And he won't look like the picture that's circulating. I'm trusting you to protect her."

"That's what I'm here for."

"Yeah, but would you die for her?"

The man raised a brow. "I don't plan on letting anyone get that close."

Seth gave a reluctant nod. "All right, then. See you soon."

Tonya bit her lip as Seth left the room, then drew in a deep breath and looked at her new friend. "All right. I guess I need to get that phone." She looked down at herself. "And dust myself off."

"That was amazing out there. I've never seen anything like it."

"Don't go to rodeos much?"

He reddened. "No, not much. But I might after today. Talk about an adrenaline rush."

She gave a short laugh. "Tell me about it."

"Let me just check the hallway." He walked to the door and opened it.

Jake and Monty tried to step inside. The officer held up a hand.

"It's all right," Tonya said. "I know these guys."

He let them pass and Tonya went to Jake and hugged him, then Monty. "Good to see you guys."

"You too, Tonya. That was crazy bullfighting out there." She smiled. "Thanks. Have either of you seen Mia?"

Jake nodded. "She was out in the hallway not too long ago talking on her cell." He grabbed a snack out of the bowl that someone had been kind enough to fill.

"Okay. Thanks." She nodded to Officer Abbott. "I'm ready when you are."

The bodyguard led the way, walking just behind her

and a little to the side so he could protect her back and see what was coming from the front.

As she walked to the dressing room, Tonya kept an eye on each doorway she passed and each person who got a little too close. Especially the men. Hank was on the loose and somebody else besides him wanted her dead. That fact was made clear by the switching of the barrels. Hank couldn't have done it. He'd escaped only thirty minutes before the show. So it had to have been someone else. Probably the same someone who'd deposited ten grand into Hank's bank account.

At the door, she paused and Officer Abbott knocked. "Anyone in there?"

"Just me." The door opened and a young barrel racer stepped out. Tonya couldn't remember her name. She was new on the circuit. The woman smiled. "And I'm leaving. You've got it all to yourself."

Officer Abbott nodded and let her pass. To Tonya he said, "Let me just check it out. Will you stand inside to the side of the door?"

"Sure." She did as he asked.

The dressing room was one of the smaller ones she'd used but big enough to meet the needs of the female participants. Her bodyguard disappeared into the back, where the toilets were. She waited for him to return, anxious to get cleaned up and out to her waiting family.

Two muffled cracks made her jerk. The thud that followed scared her. "Officer Abbott? Are you all right?"

She moved until the stalls were in sight. As well as Officer Abbott on the tiled floor and Hank Newman standing over him, his gun rising to level on her chest. "Hello again, Tonya. I knew if I waited long enough, eventually you'd show up."

TWENTY

Seth hovered next to his brother as he brought up the video. "What did you see?"

"I'm not sure. I wanted you to watch it in case you spotted something I wouldn't recognize as being out of place. Since we know the rope was cut, I was watching the video from right before you got on the bull."

Seth leaned forward. The video played and he watched. The memories washed over him. The jubilation of staying on. The horror of the slipping rope. The pain of the bull's hoof scraping his leg. The blackness. He blinked and focused. "There. I fell and Tonya and Mia did their job. There's another barrelman, too. They're all trying to distract the bull and he went after Tonya."

"There's the rope," Clay said and pointed. "See it?"

"Yeah. And that's Mia picking it up and heading out of the arena after the bull's back in his pen. She said she got it and hung it up." Seth raked a hand through his hair. "But it wasn't there when Jake went to find it."

"Right. Someone tried to throw it out."

"But who?" He tapped his chin. "Play it again. I'm missing something."

Clay rewound the video and hit Play. This time Seth refused to let the memories intrude and just focused on watching, taking in every detail. "Again."

His brother obliged.

About thirty seconds in, it hit him. "Wait. *There*. Play it in slow motion."

Again Clay did as asked and Seth sucked in a deep breath as he realized what was bothering him. "She's not supposed to be there."

Tonya stared at Hank, who now sported a bald head, black glasses and a clean-shaven face. But she knew the eyes. "You killed him," she whispered.

"I hope so. Been trying to get to you for the past few hours and he's been there every step of the way."

Tonya swallowed and tried not to let the shakes take over. "Hank, this is ridiculous. Why do you want to be with me so bad? Why do you care?"

"I don't. Not really. This time it was about the money."

"What?"

"That ten thousand you asked me about? Yeah. She gave it to me to get rid of you." His eyes hardened even more. "After all the grief you've caused me, I figured it would be my pleasure."

"She?"

"Me." Two more muffled gunshots exploded from behind her and Tonya dropped to the floor with a scream. The gun settled on the back of her head. "Now, get up."

Tonya rose to her feet, tears blinding her, betrayal raging through her. "Mia? H-how could you?" she stammered.

"It was easy." She grimaced. "Only now we've got to go."

"What about Hank?"

"Hank was always going to die. Granted, I didn't have this in mind, but my plans have been falling through since day one. It's time to change that. Now move." She jabbed the gun in Tonya's face. Tonya gasped and moved as told, praying no one would open the door.

She had no doubt that Mia would shoot anyone who walked in. Her brain raced. How was she going to get out of this? How could she overpower the other woman? Was she strong enough? Right now she was shaking so hard she wouldn't be able to open a soda, much less get a gun away from a very determined woman.

Tonya unlocked and opened the door. She glanced up the hallway, then back down. People milled, coming and going. The gun in her back said she'd better not alert them. If she did, would Mia shoot her or the person Tonya asked for help? She couldn't take any chances. She looked at the clock on the wall. The barrel racers were out there performing and the crowd was cheering.

"Where do you want me to go?" She couldn't risk asking for help.

"To my car. It's parked out back. We're going to leave the dressing room then go out the emergency exit just ahead and to the left. Understand?" Tonya paused and Mia gave her a hard shove. "Go. Or I'll come back and find every single member of your family and kill them all."

Tonya winced. She'd heard that before. This time she wasn't going to let it sway her. "Why, Mia? What did I do to you to make you do this?"

The door shut behind her and she saw the Closed—Will Reopen in 30 Minutes sign tacked to the paint. Well, that explained the lack of traffic into the dressing room. Mia had thought ahead.

"Every time I turn around, you're winning," the woman sneered. "I never get a chance, because you win every stinking competition—*and I need the money!*"

Tonya was floored. "You're jealous? You want to

kill me because you're *jealous*?" She nearly shouted the words as she pushed the door open that led out of the building. The oppressive heat hit her. She couldn't get in the car. If she did, she was dead.

She was going to have to take her chances.

"Jealous. And broke. And frustrated. I couldn't figure out how to beat you. I didn't have your death-defying acts. I couldn't wow the audience like you do or make them laugh hysterically when you get shot from the cannon to land in a pile of—"

"Stop. Just stop," Tonya hissed. Her fear was fading and anger was rising fast. "I helped you create a great routine. We worked together and you were happy. I *helped* you!"

"And it wasn't good enough, was it? Because you still won!" She lifted the weapon and opened the passenger door. "Get in and slide over behind the wheel."

The stone-cold tone sent shudders up Tonya's spine, but she did as ordered. "What do you plan to do with me?"

"You're going to disappear. It's going to look like you killed Hank and ran."

"Why would I do that? And what about the guard?"

"Ballistics will show Hank killed him. I'm not worried about that. But you and the weapon that killed Hank will never be found. You'll be a cold case years from now. And I'll be Rodeo Clown Champion from here on out. No more coming in second place. No more."

Tonya felt sick. How did one become so twisted? How had her best friend lost sight of everything that was true and right? Of the value of human life? She slid behind the driver's wheel and Mia shoved the key into the ignition. "Drive."

Tonya started the engine. "They'll watch the security cameras, you know. They'll see you forcing me to leave."

"No, they won't. I disabled the ones on this hall and outside that door."

Tonya pulled away from the emergency exit, her stomach a ball of lead. What was she going to do? Could she wreck the car? "How did you know where to find me?" She started to turn toward the main exit.

"No. Don't go that way. Turn left right here."

Tonya complied. "How did you know I'd be at Seth's family ranch?"

"The night Hank attacked you and Seth walked you over to my motor home, you stood below the window talking. I heard him mention Wrangler's Corner and having his brother investigate. When you disappeared along with Seth, Wrangler's Corner was the first place I checked. It wasn't that hard to find the Starke family ranch. Everyone knows them around here."

Of course.

"How did you find Hank?"

"Again, it wasn't hard to put two and two together. You told your story. I had Hank's name. I knew the trial would be publicized…" She shrugged. "A simple internet search and I knew all I needed to know. I sent Hank a message asking if he was still interested in knowing where Tonya *Lewis* was. He jumped on it."

"And so you threw in ten thousand to sweeten the pot. I thought you said you were broke."

"I am. That's not my money and I have to give it back before it's discovered it's missing. Ten grand is just a measly amount. I need well over ten times that and the only way to get it is to get rid of you. That ten grand is an investment that's going to pay off just as soon as you're out of the picture. I'll start winning and my troubles will be over."

"Troubles? What troubles?"

"It doesn't matter. I'm not getting into that." She smirked. "I was worried Hank wouldn't be interested anymore. But he was. He was supposed to come after you and kill you. Then I would kill him and set it up as a murder-suicide. I have the account number and banking information so I could get my money back after he was dead. Unfortunately, it didn't quite go down like that, so I'm just going to have to improvise."

"Why cut Seth's rope?" It was a stab in the dark, but she seemed to be the most logical person to have done it.

Mia raised a brow. "Why not? I could tell he cared about you. He watched you all the time, made excuses to talk to you, had his arm around you when you came to my place after getting back from the hospital." She paused. "But not only that, I could see you had feelings for him, too. Daniel was willing to die for you to protect you. I thought maybe I could make the reverse happen."

"So you were trying to kill me…and Seth was just collateral damage."

"Exactly." She cut a glance at Tonya. "I knew how torn up you would be to see another buckaroo die on your watch. I thought once the rope broke, he'd wind up under the hooves and you would get between him and the bull. But of course it didn't work that way—because *nothing* works my way—and you just wound up being the hero." Her bitterness filled the car.

Tonya thought she might throw up.

"Turn here," Mia ordered. Tonya spun the wheel and pulled up to the back gate of the arena. Once she was through that gate, she was dead. She stomped on the brake, throwing Mia forward into the dash. She hadn't put on her seat belt and neither had Tonya. Mia screamed and Tonya threw open the driver's door. She stumbled, hit the ground, then scrambled to her feet to run.

She took two steps and felt something slam into her back. She grunted and rolled.

Saw the gun coming at her head. The first blow stunned her. The second sent her spiraling down into darkness.

TWENTY-ONE

Seth's heart pounded as he stared at the sign on the door of the women's dressing room. He'd retrieved his phone, watched the video and seen Mia Addison cut his rope. It had been a subtle move. A razor blade in the palm of her hand. She looked as though she were helping. He snorted. Right, helping send him straight to his grave. She'd been dressed as a bull rider and had her hair pulled up under her hat. Her tall, wiry, boyish figure had easily passed for a male. No one had given her a second glance in the midst of getting him on the bull.

Clay noted the sign, knocked, then shoved the door open. "Tonya?"

Seth followed him. "She's not here." And Officer Abbott hadn't been answering his phone.

Clay strode toward the back, Seth on his heels. He heard Clay's indrawn breath and looked around his brother's broad shoulders. "Oh no."

Seth pulled out his phone to dial for help while Clay knelt beside the first man. "Is he alive?" Seth asked.

"Not this one." Clay moved to the police officer.

Seth spit out the information while his heart pounded with fear for Tonya. Where was she?

"He's alive," Clay breathed.

"Help's on the way." Seth grabbed paper towels from the holder and pressed against the wound in the man's shoulder. "It missed the vest. Looks like he knocked his head pretty hard on the floor when he fell." He looked closer at the other man on the floor. "That's Hank Newman."

Clay blinked. "You're right."

"If Hank's dead, who killed him?"

"This whole thing is getting more and more strange."

"We've got to find Tonya," Seth said.

The door opened and Seth bolted to his feet to wave the two EMTs in. They hurried to the wounded man and Seth stood back out of the way, then looked down at the blood on his hands. He went to the sink and scrubbed them clean while sending up prayers for Tonya's safety.

Clay came up behind him. "Mia had something to do with this."

"I think so, too. She disguised herself to gain access to me. To cut my rope. I don't know why, but in any case, we've got to find Mia."

Clay got on his phone and requested access to video cameras immediately. "Let's go—we've got more video to watch."

Seth followed Clay, his heart thumping, crazy worry racing through him. More prayers were whispered from his lips, but within minutes he found himself in the security office of the rodeo. Clay barked out what he needed and the young woman dressed in a white shirt and black pants started typing. The screens flickered. Some remained black. "What is it?" Clay demanded.

"The black screens mean something's interfering with the camera. Wait a minute. Look." She pointed toward another screen. "That camera's mounted on the pole at the gate of the back exit. There's a car leaving."

Clay leaned in. "Can you see who's in the car?"

She played with the video a bit but couldn't get a good angle. "The camera I need is one that's blocked, but…" More clicking. "There—that's the best I can do."

Seth squinted. "That's Mia in the passenger seat."

"So who's driving?" his brother asked.

She let the video footage play and Seth blinked when the brake lights came on and the driver door flew open. Tonya bolted from the car. His breath caught as she tripped over her own feet. She landed hard but didn't stop and was on her feet in less than a second. Unfortunately, Mia was already out of the car. Seth watched her slam into Tonya's back and take her down to the dirt ground.

Tonya rolled and Mia hit her twice with the weapon she'd never let go of. Tonya went still and so did Seth's heart.

"Can you get the plate?" Clay asked. Seth heard the tension in his brother's voice over the roaring in his ears. His head went light and fear like no other coursed through him. The pain of getting stomped by the bull that broke his leg was minor compared to the pain of seeing Tonya's brutal kidnapping.

The security guard nodded and let them see Mia heft Tonya into the backseat of the car. Then Mia climbed into the driver's seat and headed through the gate.

They watched the car, and the guard paused the video when she had a good shot of the back of the vehicle. Her fingers flew over the keys. The camera zoomed in. "Excellent," Clay hissed and turned to get on his phone.

Seth rubbed his eyes and prayed. Acid burned in his gut and he tried to force his petrified brain to think. Clay hung up and Seth pounced. "What do we do now?"

"I've got a BOLO out on the vehicle. Now we just pray a cop sees it and calls it in."

"Where would she go? Can you get some background on Mia? Someplace she would take Tonya if she were going to kill her?"

Clay nodded. "But that'll take a while. We need to talk to someone who knows her well enough to know where she would go."

"Monty," Seth said. "Her brother's here."

"Could he be helping her?"

Seth narrowed his eyes. "Only one way to find out." He snagged his phone and punched in Monty's speed dial number. The man didn't answer.

He tried Jake and his breath whooshed out when the buckaroo picked up. "Yeah?"

"Do you know where Monty is?"

"Um…no. Haven't seen him. Oh, wait. Said he might go back to the break room. He wanted to get online and process some orders or something."

"Thanks." Seth hung up and relayed the information.

Together he and Clay hurried out of the office while Clay got on his phone and requested his officers and other security to be on the lookout for Monty Addison.

"Okay," Seth said. He walked to the door. "I'm going to see if Monty's in the break room."

Clay nodded. "I'm coming." He grabbed Seth's shoulder. "If things get dangerous, you need to hang back. You're not a cop."

"No, I'm a man in love," he bit out. "And if she's in danger, I'm going in." He slipped out of the room, ignoring Clay's half-stunned, half-angry look. Then he heard his brother's footsteps behind him.

Seth made his way through the crowd to the other building that housed the break room. The dressing room building was closed off. Crime scene tape covered part of it. Officers still worked the area and he saw the medical examiner's vehicle at the entrance. Seth pushed into the other building and hurried down the hall and through the break room door. Monty sat on the couch with his laptop open, his brow furrowed in concentration. He was surrounded by other rodeo participants. Some lounged; some ate. All were laughing and joking.

"Monty, can you step outside for a second?" Seth asked quietly. "I need to talk to you for a minute." He bit his tongue to keep the accusations from flying from it. Monty sure didn't act as if he knew what his sister was up to.

Monty looked up from the laptop with a frown. "Sure. Hang on a sec." He clicked a few more keys, then shut the computer and handed it off to one of the other buckaroos who worked the business with him. Monty stood. "What's up?"

"Just come out in the hall, will you?"

"How long is this going to take? I've got a lot of orders to process and not a lot of time to work with."

"Shouldn't take long," Clay said.

"I hope not," Seth muttered. As soon as Monty cleared the room, Seth shut the door. "Where's Mia?"

Monty's frown deepened. "I don't know. Why?"

Clay placed a hand on Seth's arm. "I'm Clay, Seth's brother. I'm also the sheriff here in Wrangler's Corner. We need to find your sister because she's the one behind the threats on Tonya's life."

The man stared at them for a moment, then gave a hesitant chuckle. "Come on, guys. That's not funny."

"That's because it's not a joke," Seth said. "We've got her on the security video knocking Tonya out and forcing her into her car and then driving off."

Now anger surfaced on Monty's face. "Are you crazy? Mia and Tonya are best friends. I can't believe you would accuse her of that."

His nostrils flared and his fingers curled into fists at his sides. Seth thought the man might just take a swing at him. "She also wired ten thousand dollars to Hank Newman, Tonya's stalker from four years ago."

Monty snorted. "Now I *know* you're crazy. She doesn't have ten grand. If she had ten thousand dollars to hire a hit man, she would have used it to pay off debt owed—" He drew in a deep breath. "She doesn't have that kind of money."

"She got it from somewhere," Clay said. He looked up from his phone. "Actually, it was traced back to an account with your name on it."

"What?" Monty yanked his phone from his pocket. He jabbed the screen with a shaking forefinger and he studied it intently. His breathing grew rapid, and sweat dripped into his eyes. He swiped it with the back of his arm. "Oh no. No, no, no, no. She didn't. How—?" He looked up. "It's gone. Every penny," he whispered. "That's not my money. That belongs to all the guys in the business. What am I going to do?"

"We're not worried about the money right now. Where would she go?" Seth nearly shouted.

"No, she wouldn't do this." Monty ignored them, seemed able to focus only on the missing money. "How would she get access…?" He stared down at the screen again.

Several more seconds ticked by and Seth thought his head would explode. "We don't have time to try and convince him," he told Clay. "You're going to have to show Monty the video. And quick."

Clay paused, then nodded. "I have an idea." He got on his phone and Seth listened to him talk to the woman in the security booth. When he hung up, he tapped a few buttons and turned his phone so Monty could see it. She was sending the video to Clay over FaceTime.

Monty set his own phone aside and watched. The more he saw, the more he paled. At the end of the video, he swallowed hard and leaned against the wall for support. Seth placed a hand on his shoulder. "I'm sorry, man, but where would she go? We need to know. *Now*."

Monty shook his head. A tremor went through him and his hands shook. "I don't know. I don't—" He froze.

"What?" Seth demanded.

"Old Hickory Lake," Monty rasped. "That's where she would go. It's our old family lake house. It's also in foreclosure. She was supposed to use the money from winning contests to pay the back payments and taxes, but—"

"*But?*" Clay asked.

"Tonya kept winning and second place just wasn't enough." He slid down the wall as though his legs couldn't support him anymore. "Oh, my... I can't believe she'd do this."

"Let's go," Seth urged. "Time is passing."

Clay was already calling for backup. Seth grabbed Monty's arm and hauled the stunned man to his feet. "You're coming, too. You might have to talk her out of killing Tonya."

Tonya groaned, her head pounding in time to the rhythm of her heart. What happened? Had she finally been stomped by an angry bull? She groaned again and tried to sit up. Gasping at the nausea that roiled through her, she immediately stilled. Moving wasn't an option right now. She concentrated on keeping the contents of her stomach from making an appearance, closed her eyes and used her other senses to figure out where she was. Her mind struggled to focus.

She tried to move her hands and found them bound in front of her.

Fear flooded her, as well as the memories. Mia!

Mia had kidnapped her. Mia had knocked her out. Mia. Her best friend. *Oh, God, please help me! I need You...*

Her mind went to Seth. He'd be looking for her. Her family would wonder where she was, why she hadn't shown up. As she lay still thinking, she listened. Water. She heard it. She smelled it. A lake? She lifted her head and winced as dizziness hit her. She lay still again, wondering where Mia was now. Tonya didn't hear footsteps or anyone talking. She felt the hard board beneath her. Wood. Water lapping against something. A dock?

She opened her eyes and blinked against the brightness. She vaguely realized her symptoms mimicked the concussion she'd had the time she'd fallen out of the tree when she was ten.

Great.

Fear wanted to paralyze her and make her tremble all at the same time. She let her eyes roam her immediate surroundings. The lake out beyond the dock. The sinking sun...but it wouldn't be dark for another hour or so.

How would she get loose? She tried to pull but the rope was too tight. Mia knew how to tie her knots. Tonya rolled to her back with a grunt. Lightning arched through her head and tears leaked down her temples into her ears. *Please, God, please.*

She didn't know how long she lay there staring at the metal roof, but the day was coming to an end, the setting sun slipping down toward the horizon with every breath she took.

She braced herself and tried to sit up. She managed it

and had to close her eyes and hold herself still until the nausea passed. But at least it did.

"Well, well, look who's awake. You should have stayed out of it another few minutes and you'd never have known what hit you. Or how you're going to die."

TWENTY-TWO

Seth sat in the front of Clay's cruiser as the man raced down the highway toward Old Hickory Lake. He kept his eyes on the road in front of him and prayed for Tonya's safety. He really did love her. He'd said it out loud, but the words didn't do the emotion justice. He loved her like he'd love no other. Probably had for a while. But because of Glory's betrayal, he'd closed himself off from his feelings. Only to be drawn to Tonya, who was as afraid of commitment as he was.

If he hadn't been so scared, he would have smiled at the irony. "How much longer?"

"Not long," Monty said. "Coming up on the turn. Watch for it."

"Are the local cops there yet?"

Clay kept his left hand on the wheel and checked his phone with his other. "Yes. Just getting there."

"Why would Mia do this?" Seth asked hoarsely. "Why?"

"Money," Monty sighed. "It's always about money. We never had any as kids. Our daddy was a buckaroo wannabe. Traveled the circuit while our mama stayed home working in the local diner. Mia hated it. Couldn't wait to get out." He cleared his throat. "Then our daddy died, got killed getting thrown off a bull. Broke his neck. Mama left us with the social worker and disappeared. Ain't seen her since."

Seth couldn't imagine growing up like that. His heart almost softened for the two lost souls who deserved a much better childhood. "What about the lake house?"

"That's been our refuge. Mama's cousin took us in. I was fifteen and Mia was seventeen. She loved that place. We lived there for a couple of years before we both joined up with the rodeo. Jerry and Paula got a divorce and put the house up for sale. Mia managed to get the loan to buy the house but couldn't keep up the payments once Tonya joined the rodeo and started winning prize money left and right. I've managed to help with the payments some, but—" he sighed "—the online business isn't doing as well as we would have liked. That ten thousand dollars is already spent. And then some." He rubbed his eyes. "It was all crashing down around us."

"So she blames Tonya," Seth said.

"Apparently," Monty said, his voice shaking. "The house is in foreclosure and Mia is desperate to save it."

"Why didn't she just use the ten grand to pay on the house instead of hiring someone to kill Tonya?" Seth growled.

"Ten thousand dollars is a mere drop in the bucket," Monty moaned. "She started gambling. She was going to have to sell the house to pay the bookie, but then she kept falling further and further behind on the payments because she kept losing…" He bit his lip and glanced out the window. "If we lose that house, we lose everything. Her winnings were supposed to— It's a mess. I can't believe she's resorted to this."

"Believe it. Because Tonya's life is hanging by a thread."

* * *

Tonya hung on to consciousness as Mia gripped her arms and dragged her toward the canoe she'd released from the boathouse and tied to the dock. Mia grunted and lost her grip. Tonya rolled. Mia kicked her in the ribs and Tonya curled into a ball, fighting the pain and nausea. The descending darkness. "Stop, Mia. Stop!"

Sirens split the air and Mia froze. Tonya panted and relief flooded her. "You better run. They know where you are. They know I'm here and they're coming for me. Get out while you can."

"Nice try. There's no way anyone knows anything."

The sirens grew louder. "You messed up. You missed something. Somehow they put it together and they know." She inched away from Mia back toward the land. Away from the boat. She had to buy herself some time.

Mia glanced in the direction of the sirens. Tonya could see the lights winking through the trees. Mia whirled back toward her, the gun aimed in her direction. Without hesitation, Tonya lifted her legs and shot them out to catch Mia in the midsection. The gun spun from her fingers, skidding across the dock into the water. Mia finally gasped in air and let it back out on a scream of rage. "I hate you! Why did you have to show up and ruin my life?"

Tonya didn't bother with an answer. She scooted as fast as she could away from the water, rolled to her stomach and army-crawled. Splinters pricked at her elbows. And then her ankles were snared in a vise grip. "Fine. If I can't shoot you, I can at least drown you."

"There's no point now, Mia! They know!"

"No, they don't!" Spittle flew from her lips and Tonya was helpless to stop the woman from dragging her back toward the water.

"Tonya!"

She wiggled and bucked and kicked. "Seth!" she screamed.

Mia wailed and with a mighty heave pushed Tonya over the side of the dock.

Seth saw Tonya roll into the water, heard her muffled cry cut off as she slipped beneath the surface. Vaguely he registered Clay's hollers for him to stop. He ignored them all. He saw Mia untie the canoe from the dock and jump in. She was Clay's to deal with; he was going after Tonya. Seth hit the water at the exact spot he saw her roll off and felt it close over him. He held his breath and reached out, grasping, desperate to feel her, to find her. He opened his eyes and could see nothing but darkness. Terror threatened to close in on him.

Then his fingers brushed something. His lungs started to protest the lack of air. But he couldn't stop now. He might lose her. His heart thumped, his blood pulsed and his lungs ached.

One more reach.

Hair. Her hair. He snagged his fingers in it and pulled it toward him. Yes, hair attached to Tonya's beloved head. With his other hand, he felt for her face, touched her nose. He moved his hand down and shoved it under her armpit. Then he kicked hard and shot them toward the surface.

He broke through and gasped. He turned Tonya toward him, opened her mouth and placed his lips over hers. He blew. Once. Twice. She sputtered, coughed and threw up the water she'd swallowed.

Seth let a sob escape and didn't care. He trod water and held her as best he could against his chest. "Tonya. Tonya, talk to me. Oh, honey, I'm so sorry."

She drew in a ragged breath and he kicked again, this time toward the dock or land. Whichever came first. A choked cry escaped her and he missed what she said. "What?"

She cleared her throat. "You saved my life."

"I owed you." He touched bottom and planted his feet as he cradled her against him.

"Yeah. You did. You owe me one more, but I'm not going to hold you to it. I'd rather not need it." Her voice croaked and the tears came.

He heard some commotion behind him but didn't move. She felt so right in his arms. So alive. His grip tightened. "I told you so."

"What?"

"I told you it would be all right."

She let out a hiccupy chuckle. "Yes, you did. Thank God."

"Definitely. We're going to be thanking God for the rest of our lives."

She stilled. "We are?"

"Yes, but we'll talk about that later." He sighed ruefully. Standing at the edge of a lake with the water lapping around their legs might sound romantic in some settings, but not this one. She still had her wrists and legs bound. "Hey, I need a knife!"

He hefted her into his arms and gave a test step. His leg twinged but held, and soon he had her onshore. An officer passed him a knife and he freed her arms and legs. She gasped as the blood started flowing again, then threw her arms around his neck. "Thank you," she whispered against the base of his throat.

He kissed the top of her head. "You're very welcome."

She drew in a shuddering breath. "Where's Mia?"

He looked around and saw the bedraggled, wet woman being led to a police cruiser by an equally soaking-wet

Clay. Her hands were cuffed behind her. "Looks like she tried to swim to freedom."

Tonya stared at her former friend and would-be murderer. "But Clay got her."

"Yep. I went for you—he went for her."

Tonya pushed away from him. "Clay, wait."

Clay paused and leaned Mia against the car as he turned to face her. "Yes?"

"Thank you."

"You're welcome."

She looked at Mia, hurt and confusion and anger blazing in her eyes. Mia stared back, shoulders slumped but defiance in every line of her body. "You betrayed me. You tried to kill me because of money and jealousy."

"You should have just left. If you had only run when you knew Hank was after you, none of this would have happened. But no, you had to choose *this* time to stay and fight. I hope you're miserable the rest of your life!" she spit at Tonya.

Tonya's fist cut through the air at the speed of light and connected with Mia's jaw. The woman never made a sound. Her eyes rolled back in her head and she started to sink to the ground. Clay caught her and looked at Tonya with a brow raised, surprise and a glint of admiration lighting his gaze. Seth thought his brother might say something but he didn't. He just pushed Mia into the cruiser and fastened her seat belt for her.

"That was a mean right hook," Seth murmured.

"Grant would be proud." She touched her knuckles and winced. "Now I need an ice pack and a shower and a nap."

Seth pulled her to face him. "I love you, Tonya." She froze and let her gaze stay trapped on his. He placed a finger on her lips. "I know you're leery of commitment to another bull rider after what happened with Daniel, but I don't want to lose you." He drew in a deep breath and blew it out slowly. "I'll quit."

She gasped. "No. Oh no, Seth, that's your passion, your love, your calling. You can't say that."

He shook his head. "No, you're my passion, my love. I care more about building a future with you than I do the rodeo. And if quitting is what it takes, that's what I'll do." Tonya shivered and Seth ran his hands up and down her arms. She leaned her head against his chest and he nodded to the hovering EMTs. "Let's get you checked out. The rest of this can wait until later."

She allowed herself to be ushered into the back of the ambulance and once again she was whisked away from him.

He just prayed it wasn't forever.

Tonya received the all clear from the hospital. She had been under for only a short time. Long enough to inhale some water, not long enough to do any permanent damage. She was exhausted and kept her eyes closed as she relaxed against the hospital bed pillow. Her family had already come and gone and now Seth was here and waiting to see her.

Grant had gone to find him.

What would she say? His words still echoed in her mind. She hadn't been able to think of anything else, not the fact that she was now free to resume a normal life, free to stop running, free to be Tonya Lewis. She was free. And she knew she'd keep doing exactly what she'd been doing the past four years. Only now she didn't have to keep looking over her shoulder.

She could settle down with a man who loved her.

Seth. Just thinking his name sent goose bumps rippling up her arms. *God, I think I love him, too, and I'm so scared he could die and—*

"Tonya?"

Her eyes flew open. And there he was, standing at her bedside, looking strong and healthy and oh, so very handsome—but with a worried frown creasing the area between his brows. Peace settled in her heart. She was still scared, but she knew what she wanted. "I want that, too."

He blinked. "What?"

"I want a future with you and I don't want you to give up bull riding." She held out a hand and his eyes filled with hope and a sheen of tears. "I don't want you to quit. I want you to go out there and be the best bull rider you can be. And I'm going to be the best bullfighter. We've been a team for a long time on the rodeo circuit. Why mess with a good thing?" She felt the tears slip down her cheeks and sniffed.

Seth picked up her hand and kissed her bruised knuckles. "Are you sure?"

"I'm sure." She smiled. "You promised me it would be all right, remember? I believe you."

He gave a shaky laugh and then leaned over and kissed her softly, cherishing her, telling her how much her words meant to him. Loving her. When he pulled away, she protested, but he caught her hands. "I know it's fast and I know it's crazy, but I don't want a long engagement."

She blinked. "Was that a marriage proposal?"

He closed his eyes and winced. "I'm an idiot. I didn't do it right. I don't have flowers and candy or fancy words, but yes, it's a proposal."

She sniffed back tears and reached up to cup his cheek. "I don't need flowers or candy or fancy words. I just need you." He kissed her again.

When he pulled back, he groaned. "You know if you

tell my mother how I went about asking you to marry me, she's going to have my hide. She'll write me out of the will. She'll—"

She placed a finger over his lips. "Shh. Your mom loves me, Seth. Trust me…" She smiled and kept her gaze locked on his. "It'll be all right."

EPILOGUE

Six months later
National Finals Rodeo
Las Vegas, NV

Tonya waited at the gate while Seth settled himself on the back of the bull. He'd made it. He'd been number fifteen in the lineup, but he'd made it into the finals and she was so proud. Her heart thudded and her adrenaline flowed as it always did. Butterflies swarmed in her belly and she pressed a hand against her middle. She couldn't deny that twinge of worry, that niggling of fear that she felt just before the gates opened.

But she trusted him. He was doing what he was called to do. And so was she. He caught her eye and blew her a kiss. She flushed under the makeup and the crowd cheered. The ring on her finger glinted under the lights, winking at her, a symbol of their love made complete by marriage. They'd become the circuit's rodeo sweethearts, and right now Seth was milking it for all it was worth. Tonya had to admit she didn't mind. It was a brief moment in time. A short fun stint that would eventually end, but there was no reason not to let everyone have their fun while it lasted.

She drew in a deep breath, said a short prayer and rubbed her palms down her jeans. There were four bull-fighters in the arena for this ride and most people wouldn't question it. Three was the usual number, but Tonya had a reason for the extra person.

And now it was time. She and the bullfighter opposite her pulled the gates open. The angry animal shot out into the arena and Tonya let the other three bullfighters go to work. They stayed with the bull and her favorite rider, dancing out of reach of the hooves but ready to run in and intervene should he need it.

Seth rode, one hand wrapped tight, the other flung up beside him. The bull spun, bucked and landed hard. But Seth stayed on, his seat a good one, his grip strong like iron. She forced the air in and out of her lungs, knowing that holding her breath was not an option. *Breathe, Tonya, breathe.* The crowd roared; the clock ticked down.

And still Seth stayed on.

Three…two…one.

The buzzer sounded and Seth waited for the bull to land one more time before jumping off at the most opportune moment he could find.

The bullfighter to her right burst into action. She slapped the bull on his hindquarters and he spun from Seth to her. The other bullfighter distracted the animal and made it over the fence. A rope dropped over the bull's neck and he was led back to the pen. The crowd continued to roar and clap.

She raced to the rail, up and over and into her husband's arms. "You did it!" Four months she'd been married to this man and sometimes she had to pinch herself to believe it.

He lifted her up and swung her around, then planted a kiss on her upturned lips. "Yep. It was a good ride."

"Are you kidding? It was as close to perfect as you could get."

He cupped her chin. "What was the deal out there? You were hanging back, letting the other three work the bull."

She grinned. "That's because I've got a surprise for you and I couldn't take any chances on getting hurt this time around."

He frowned. "What do you mean?"

"Look at the screen."

His brows furrowed. He shot her a wary look but did as she asked and turned to look.

Tonya lifted a hand and gave the announcer in the box a thumbs-up.

The screen flashed and the picture she'd taken early that morning hung suspended above the crowd. Seth gasped. The crowd roared and rose to their feet. The noise level was deafening, so she didn't even try to speak. The tears clogging her throat prevented it anyway.

The announcer waited. Finally, he began to speak. "All of us at the National Finals Rodeo offer our most sincere congratulations to Seth and Tonya Starke as they antic-ipate the arrival of their firstborn sometime this fall."

Once again the decibel level rose. Seth simply stared at the screen. The picture of the pregnancy stick with the double lines posted there for all to see. Then he whooped and threw his hat into the air. He grabbed Tonya and bur-ied his face against her neck. The screen flickered and she saw the camera was on them, sharing their joy with their rodeo family.

She clung to him and his grip tightened. Then he dropped to his knees to plant a kiss on her still-flat belly. He looked up, tears streaming down his rugged cheeks. "I love you, Mrs. Starke."

"And I love you, Mr. Starke."

"You're a crazy woman to announce it this way."

"Are you mad?"

"Mad about you. This is pure genius. What a story we already have to tell our kid." He flashed a grin. "And bless her, but now my mother will totally be over the whole way I asked you to marry me."

She laughed and pulled him to his feet for another sweet kiss. The announcer was talking, but no one was paying attention. The crowd was enraptured by the best show a rodeo clown had ever performed.

Tonya sent up a silent prayer of thanks for the way everything had turned out.

He kissed her ear. "Told you everything would be all right."

And it definitely was.

* * * * *

Dear Reader,

I hope you've enjoyed this second installment of the Wrangler's Corner series. I had a lot of fun researching rodeos and bull riders and bullfighters. I watched several rodeos and interviewed numerous rodeo participants to make the story as realistic as possible. Truthfully, it would be very hard for someone to really sabotage the rope of a bull rider, but I took some artistic license in order to make the story work. Thank you for allowing me to do that. Seth and Tonya both had quite a bit of emotional baggage to deal with even while they found themselves falling in love. Tonya came to understand that God was there for her no matter what, and Seth came to realize that he couldn't fully rely on himself to keep Tonya safe. Only God could do that. But they were a team and by working together were able to defeat evil and find their happily-ever-after. I pray if you're facing a hardship, you will place your troubles in God's hands and trust Him to lead you out of the valley and onto the mountaintop.

Until next time,

Lynette Eason

REQUEST YOUR FREE BOOKS!

2 FREE RIVETING INSPIRATIONAL NOVELS
PLUS 2 FREE MYSTERY GIFTS

Love Inspired®

SUSPENSE
RIVETING INSPIRATIONAL ROMANCE

YES! Please send me 2 FREE Love Inspired® Suspense novels and my 2 FREE mystery gifts (gifts are worth about $10). After receiving them, if I don't wish to receive any more books, I can return the shipping statement marked "cancel." If I don't cancel, I will receive 4 brand-new novels every month and be billed just $4.99 per book in the U.S. or $5.49 per book in Canada. That's a savings of at least 17% off the cover price. It's quite a bargain! Shipping and handling is just 50¢ per book in the U.S. and 75¢ per book in Canada.* I understand that accepting the 2 free books and gifts places me under no obligation to buy anything. I can always return a shipment and cancel at any time. Even if I never buy another book, the two free books and gifts are mine to keep forever.

123/323 IDN GH5Z

Name _____ (PLEASE PRINT) _____

Address _____ Apt. # _____

City _____ State/Prov. _____ Zip/Postal Code _____

Signature (if under 18, a parent or guardian must sign) _____

Mail to the **Reader Service:**
IN U.S.A.: P.O. Box 1867, Buffalo, NY 14240-1867
IN CANADA: P.O. Box 609, Fort Erie, Ontario L2A 5X3

**Are you a current subscriber to Love Inspired® Suspense books
and want to receive the larger-print edition?
Call 1-800-873-8635 or visit www.ReaderService.com.**

* Terms and prices subject to change without notice. Prices do not include applicable taxes. Sales tax applicable in N.Y. Canadian residents will be charged applicable taxes. Offer not valid in Quebec. This offer is limited to one order per household. Not valid for current subscribers to Love Inspired Suspense books. All orders subject to credit approval. Credit or debit balances in a customer's account(s) may be offset by any other outstanding balance owed by or to the customer. Please allow 4 to 6 weeks for delivery. Offer available while quantities last.

Your Privacy—The Reader Service is committed to protecting your privacy. Our Privacy Policy is available online at www.ReaderService.com or upon request from the Reader Service.
We make a portion of our mailing list available to reputable third parties that offer products we believe may interest you. If you prefer that we not exchange your name with third parties, or if you wish to clarify or modify your communication preferences, please visit us at www.ReaderService.com/consumerchoice or write to us at Reader Service Preference Service, P.O. Box 9062, Buffalo, NY 14240-9062. Include your complete name and address.

LIS15

SPECIAL EXCERPT FROM

Will a young Amish widow's life change when her brother-in-law arrives unexpectedly at her farm?

Read on for a sneak preview of
THE AMISH MOTHER
The second book in the brand-new trilogy
LANCASTER COURTSHIPS

"You're living here with the children," Zack said. *"Alone?"*

"This is our home." Lizzie faced him, a petite woman whose auburn hair suddenly appeared as if streaked with various shades of reds under the autumn sun. Her vivid green eyes and young, innocent face made her seem vulnerable, but she must be a strong woman if she could manage all seven of his nieces and nephews—and stand defiantly before him as she was now without backing down. He felt a glimmer of admiration for her.

"*Koom.* We're about to have our midday meal. Join us. You must have come a long way." She bit her lip as she briefly met his gaze.

Zack still couldn't believe that Abraham was dead. His older brother had been only thirty-five years old. "What happened to my *brooder*?"

Lizzie went pale. "He fell," she said in a choked voice, "from the barn loft." He saw her hands clutch at the hem of her apron. "He broke his neck and died instantly."

Zack felt shaken by the mental image. "I'm sorry. I know it's hard." He, too, felt the loss. It hurt to realize that he'd never see Abraham again.

"He was a *goot* man." She didn't look at him when she bent to pick up her basket, then straightened. "Are you coming in?" she asked as she finally met his gaze.

He nodded and then followed her as she started toward the house. He was surprised to see her uneven gait as she walked ahead of him, as if she'd injured her leg and limped because of the pain. "Lizzie, are *ya* hurt?" he asked compassionately.

She halted, then faced him with her chin tilted high, her eyes less than warm. "I'm not hurt," she said crisply. "I'm a cripple." And with that, she turned away and continued toward the house, leaving him to follow her.

Zack studied her back with mixed feelings. Concern. Worry. Uneasiness. He frowned as he watched her struggle to open the door. He stopped himself from helping, sensing that she wouldn't be pleased. Could a crippled, young nineteen-year-old woman raise a passel of *kinner* alone?

Don't miss
THE AMISH MOTHER by Rebecca Kertz,
available October 2015 wherever
Love Inspired® books and ebooks are sold.